RICHARD WORMSER

◆

PERFECT PIGEON

9 013448686

Complete and Unabridged

LINFORD
Leicester

First published in Great Britain

First Linford Edition
published 2018

A catalogue record for this book is available
from the British Library.

ISBN 978–1–4448–3733–9

Published by
F. A. Thorpe (Publishing)
Anstey, Leicestershire

Set by Words & Graphics Ltd.
Anstey, Leicestershire
Printed and bound in Great Britain by
T. J. International Ltd., Padstow, Cornwall

This book is printed on acid-free paper

1

In the six years I had been in the place, I had never gotten closer than thirty feet to the warden. Now I stood face to face with him; he reached out and shook hands with me. 'You've been a good prisoner, Daniels,' he said. My name was Mark Daniels, then.

I muttered some kind of thanks. 'Six years without a mark,' he said. 'It's kind of a record. But we don't get many so bright as you. Criminals with brains are rare.'

'Either they're rare,' I said, 'or they don't get caught.'

He gave me a sort of startled look. I was wearing my own clothes that I'd worn into prison so long ago, but I was still technically a prisoner. He expected respect, even awe from me; the awe he always got in his little world of convicts and guards.

After a moment, he shrugged. 'Daniels,'

he said. Then he grinned. 'Mr. Daniels, here's the five dollars the state says I have to give you. I suppose you won't need it.'

'That makes two thousand and five I've got,' I said. 'The two grand was left me by an uncle, just before I came here.'

He laughed. 'How about the quarter of a million you took from the bank?'

There was a window in his office; barred, of course, but still a window. Our cell blocks were set in the middle of a huge hall. The windows were forty feet away; the library, the laundry and the school buildings where I'd worked at various times in my six years all had windows, but they opened onto prison yards. This window looked out at the free world. I looked out of it.

The warden said, 'I suppose if you held out for six years, you'd not be likely to tell me now. Still . . . ' He sighed.

'The money was in an old carpetbag,' I said. 'I fell asleep on a bus and when I woke up, it was gone.'

'I know, I know. I read the papers, too. And talking about papers, it'll start again the minute you get outside the gate.

There's a mob of reporters waiting for you.'

'Warden, isn't there any way — '

He waved it off. 'Only one front gate to this pen. You go through it, just like any other con.' Then he relaxed. 'I could phone for a cab for you, though. You're on your own, getting from the gate to the taxi.'

'Here goes my five bucks. You couldn't cash a check?'

The warden looked at me. As he reached for the phone, he rocked with laughter. 'I've let a lot of the boys out,' he said, 'but you're the first embezzler who ever asked me that.' He was still laughing as he dialed the cab company.

★　★　★

The reporters weren't too bad. The me that was Mark Daniels was accustomed to reciting the carpetbag story. Mark Daniels even took pride in it. Who'd ever seen a carpetbag, unless it was on a stage or in a museum? It was a nice touch; a stolen briefcase would have been corny.

And the reporters could say no more to Mark Daniels than the warden had. In that state, embezzlement copped one to ten years, and good time cut that ten years down to six and a bit.

I, as Mark Daniels, had served my six and a bit, and nothing further could be done to me. If any man, woman or child followed me, harassed me, or interfered with my personal liberty, I could call a policeman.

Fat chance. Any cop called would be as anxious to find that quarter of a million as anyone else. Everyone else. Mark Daniels felt he had the eyes of the world on him, and it was no delusion. Title had not passed to him on the two hundred and fifty thousand; if he was caught with it, it would be taken away.

But I couldn't go to prison again for taking it, not as Mark Daniels or as anyone else. I'd read my law very carefully before making my snitch. Six years was no great time to spend earning that kind of money, and no living expenses while I earned it. I was now twenty-nine years old, and rich — if I could get to my stash without being caught.

I told myself, riding the train north, that I must cut out using words like 'stash.' Convict words.

The train north was a good dodge. Of course, the newspapermen followed me to the station. But I'd asked to be released just when two trains were in the little country stop at one time: one south, to the city where I'd been convicted and to which the warden, as his duty bound him, had given me a ticket; and one north. I waited till both were moving, and swung on to the northbound train. I'd planned this for six years and some months. The reporters were left behind, and those who tried to outfox me by hiding on the southbound cars were not only left behind but were rapidly being carried in the wrong direction.

The conductor sold me a ticket to the nearest northern city for a dollar eighty. My cab had been seventy-five cents, and big-hearted Mark Daniels had tipped a quarter. Now I had two twenty left. Plus, of course, my two thousand from Uncle

Wilson. Plus, of course, my quarter of a million.

The smoker seemed the best place for me. I still had part of a deck of cigarettes bought at the prison canteen. But before I'd smoked the first one, I got sick to my stomach. It was the first time in over six years that I had moved by anything but my own legs. I hadn't been in a car, train, buggy or wheelchair in all that time, and I'd forgotten how to keep my stomach in place when it wanted to be left behind.

So I staggered into the smelly little men's room and threw up. I kept this up till the conductor garbled the name of the little town I was going to, and then I staggered out on the platform, hoping the conductor hadn't seen me. I had used up only ninety-four cents of the dollar-eighty ticket.

The sun was shining; it was spring. As I passed a cheap railroad-station kind of bar, the smell of beer came out to me; I hadn't had a drink in a long time. But the train had scared me. Maybe one beer would make me drunk, and the bank wouldn't give me my money. I had to get going.

The teller at the bank was a woman; she looked startlingly beautiful to me, but then any woman would have. I had been too sick on the train to notice if there were any passengers who were young and female. She looked at the check, at my signature; I was now Lawrence Rankin. She went through a door, and I knew she was checking; I'd worked in a bank once myself. Then she came out of the back room and went over to a man sitting at a desk behind a railing — the vice-president and cashier, no doubt; it was a very small bank. He looked at a couple of papers she held out to him: my check, and the signature card I'd signed when I put Uncle Wilson's money there. Then he shrugged; there was nothing they could do about it. That was why I had put my money in a checking account, and lost six years' interest; a savings account can be held up thirty days, though banks seldom avail themselves of the time.

Little Miss Teller came back and got behind her grill and fed me my two grand, just the way I wanted it: thirty-nine fifties and the rest in small bills. Her hands were quick and graceful, and incredibly white-looking, with pink fingernails. I wanted to reach through the grill and grab one. I needed a woman in a very urgent way; every newly released con does.

There was no use changing my name again in that little town. If the people in the bank saw my picture in the paper and made me out as Mark Daniels, the used-car salesman would be questioned, too. So I bought the car as Peter Steen — a good used car, only two years old — and drove it out of there in a nice zigzag pattern that took me across a state line and to a state capital before closing time in the license bureau. Then I endorsed my ownership blank to Lawrence Rankin, signed Peter Steen's signature, and got a new license and new plates at the state capital. I'd planned this a long time. This was one of the states that doesn't require a driver's test; I got my driving license in the next office, and was on my way to building up the wallet full of identification that a modern man needs.

Then I drove over another state line. It was dark by now, but I kept going until my cross-countrying put me on a freeway. Then I followed it into the city Jerry Quarry had told me to meet him in. The freeway fence ended, and I got into the right-hand lane, looking for the motel Jerry had mentioned. I knew its name, of course; in my last week at the pen, every con and trusty — it seemed to me — had passed me messages from Jerry.

When I found the place, it looked good. As I read the word, it was not a hangout, but a legit motel. But Jerry Quarry had wanted to be sure he could get to me if the law put heat on the phone he was standing by.

I paid out for the best room they had; I wanted a trap to lure a pigeon into. Very posh indeed, but only ten dollars a night.

There was a sort of small night club in the front of the place, and a package store. I bought a bottle of scotch for the room and had a long, luxurious drink. Then I bathed, alone for the first time in years, and counted my money. Three hundred and no dollars and eighty-two cents, as we used to say in the bank.

2

There wasn't as much of it as I'd hoped. Cars had gone up while I'd been away, or maybe my memory was faulty. I dressed again and left two hundred and fifty bucks in the motel manager's safe; that one drink had confirmed my suspicion that my capacity was way down. Then I used the phone booth outside the motel entrance and made my call.

Jerry Quarry said, 'Stay where you are. I'll take off and get this trick set up. There's a restaurant in the Union Station, and we could have coffee there Monday morning at eleven.'

'Monday? I'd like to get rolling right now.'

He laughed over the long-distance wire. 'It'll take you till then to get all your ashes hauled,' he said, 'if you're anything like me when I finish a bit.'

'Six and a bit for me,' I said.

'Danny, you're a kick. I know how long

11

it was. We'll turn a trick before the week's out; it's good to hear from you.'

It was good to find Jerry at the same number he'd given me when he left our home away from home a year ago. His stability assured me. If he said we'd make money in a week, I could stop worrying about my dwindling bank roll.

The manager said he wouldn't advise eating in the cocktail lounge this late. 'Nothing on but a sandwich chef after nine. The coffee shop down the highway's okay.'

I walked. Driving my car hadn't been as big a strain as riding on the train, but it had been a strain. Traffic, even on the side roads I'd used, seemed to have speeded up while I was resting; and the last ten miles on the freeway had been like some kind of torture invented by a genius.

There were tables in the coffee shop, but I sat at the counter. I ordered fried shrimps, the only thing on the menu that I hadn't eaten during my stretch. When I'd been a teacher, some of my students had worked in the prisoners' kitchen, and they'd invite me over for a steak now and then. The pen bought whole carcasses of beef, and the butchers held out the filets for themselves and the mess hall gang. But shrimps never make the big house.

I drank coffee while I waited, and the scotch quieted down enough for me to feel just right. There was a man behind the counter instead of a woman; it was probably a good thing if I was to concentrate on my dinner. He brought my shrimp, fried nicely golden, with french fries on the side and a tomato sliced on lettuce and dabbed with mayonnaise. The motel man had been right; this was a good place to eat. Or maybe any place is a good place to eat your first meal out of the pen.

The counterman watched me wolfing away. When I finished, he said, 'You really can scoff, pal. Dessert?'

The word should have warned me — 'scoff' is a prison word for food — but, or so I'd heard, sailors use it, too. I said, 'Apple pie a la mode?'

'Done and done.' He turned away, got the slab of pie from a fly-proof case, and scooped up vanilla ice cream. He almost gave it to me, then turned back and added another half-scoop of ice cream and a strip of yellow cheese. He refilled my cup, saying, 'On the house.' Then he looked over his shoulder, at the cook visible through the serving window. 'Just out, mate?'

The warmth went out of the coffee, the savor from the pie. My appetite was gone. 'This morning,' I said.

'The square johns are rough here,' he said. He was making noise, but his lips weren't moving. Well, I could do that, too. We all could. 'It's no burg for a trick.'

'I know. I'm just going to blow off steam here.'

He nodded. He looked down at my dessert and frowned. I forced myself to eat it; he'd meant to be nice to me. But I didn't see how he'd spotted me. The clothes were my own; the haircut was by a union barber up for common gambling; the screws had let us have all the sunshine we needed. But this ex-con had hailed me as brother on one look.

I washed the last of the pie down with coffee and reached for my wallet. 'Here comes your good time,' my friend said. 'Take another cuppa, and scout it out. I wisht I wasn't on to midnight.'

He was looking over my shoulder as he talked; and now outdoor air moved the smoke swirls in the kitchen, high heels clattered on the tile floor, and a woman swung herself up on a stool two down from me. She said, 'Coffee, black and hot.'

My colleague said, 'Done and done,' and made his easy turn to the coffee machine. He was as at home behind a counter as behind bars.

She slipped off a doeskin gauntlet and got cigarettes out of an alligator bag. I had the match lit before the cigarette was in her mouth; she accepted the light and gave me a thanks without looking at me. She rested one elbow on the counter so the cigarette would be convenient, and took a long pull.

The counterman had a good eye. This was the real magoo — class, shape, features and complexion; hairdo, hat, and the textile quality and cut of her clothes were all just right. So was the age: about twenty-five, neither too young nor too faded. I put money on the counter, freeing myself for quick action.

When the coffee went down in front of her, steam twisting up to her face, she hoisted it with one swing and swallowed it, her throat moving twice. Then she threw a quarter from the alligator onto the plastic countertop and slid off the stool carelessly, her nylon knees flashing.

Nifty and swifty me, I got the door open for her. She went out ahead of me, and I turned, winked at the counterman, and was in the night with her.

She said, 'Thanks, but don't try to pick me up. I'm not in the mood.'

'Why not?' I asked. There was no sense in denying I'd been on the make. 'It reads like this,' I said. 'There's a cocktail lounge two places down the road, floor show and all. Maybe it's good; I've never been inside. We have one drink, and you say if you want another. If not, you get up and walk out.'

She looked at me. 'That's not much fun for your money.'

'Neither is drinking alone.'

She stared, and then slowly nodded. In the light from the lunch counter, the brim of her hat made a fine swooping line down her face. 'What did your pal in there say? Done and done.'

'I'll meet you there.' I started to walk away.

She laughed suddenly, as though she hadn't meant to. 'I'll drive you down. Get in the car. I don't have to play it *that* safe.'

Her car was a receipt for about five thousand dollars. I didn't look at the plates, but the ashtray was overflowing; she'd come a long way.

We didn't say anything on the way to the Blue Goose, which was the name of my lady-trap. We didn't have time to; the car never got itself in high gear. She parked with finesse, and I got around to put my fingers under her elbow to help her out. This time she was discreet with her skirt; an admission that she knew I was there now.

A tall and overweight lady with her bleach-job piled high on her head piloted us through the innards of the Blue Goose to a little booth. A three-man orchestra was playing something from the blue-water-and-flying-fish country.

A skinny lady with her black dye-job pulled straight back stood over our table in a tight imitation-silk blouse and a skirt cut short to show her knock-knees. My catch said, 'Scotch and water.'

In honor of the music I said, '*Dos, por favor*,' and when eyebrows crawled towards the black hair, interpreted, 'Likewise.'

Miss Class looked around and said: 'You said you'd never been here before. I admire you for it.'

Actually, to me the joint wasn't all that crummy. It was certainly a step up from where I'd spent the night before. But I said, 'It'll do.'

She was still carrying the cigarette she'd lit in the coffee shop. She snubbed it out in an ashtray that was shaped like a blue goose some amateur butcher had gutted from the top, and said, 'Aren't you going to ask me to dance?'

'Not in the agreement,' I said. 'You're entitled to one drink before I make you

18

any more offers. Such as a dance or a second drink.'

'A man of honor. A gentleman of his word. But break your lifelong rule and offer me a cigarette.'

'You smoke too much.'

'I'm too nervous.'

The black-haired waitress came with our drinks and stood over me till I'd laid down a five and gotten one back; the Blue Goose was not a trusting bird.

Miss Class looked at me, and then at the eyes under the black hair. 'Hold it, miss,' she said. She raised her highball and did to it what she had done to the scalding cup of coffee. I have never seen a throat as efficient as hers. 'Now,' she said, 'you are released from your oath, Sir Knight.'

'Have another.'

'With pleasure.'

I waved the waitress away with two fingers and added, 'And a dance. And my heart.'

'Too late. Oh God, how too late. For the dance, I mean.'

She was right, sigh, expletive and all.

The lights on the dance floor were changing; the two couples who had been dancing were leaving; and the hostess, holding up strongly under her hairdo, was marching out to take up her position in front of the three-man band. They slowed their rhythm, dropped their volume, and were led by their lady general into a rendition of 'All of Me.' When there were no takers, Miss Piled-high took a deep breath and changed into 'A Good Man is Hard to Find,' from experience.

The waitress swapped fresh glasses for four more of my dollars, and Miss Class said, 'Cheers, thanks, and my name is Colomba.'

'Columbia?'

'Colomba. Latin for pigeon, and who knows but what my learned mother chose wisely.'

This was going as fast as I could have hoped. There was nothing to do but take it easy; I gave her my first name, which was Larry at the moment, and we waited till the thrush got through 'Body and Soul' — bruising both of them — and then we danced.

Astaire had never had anything to envy me for up till now, but with Colomba I was pretty darned smooth, if I say it myself, who was the only other witness.

Twenty dollars and maybe four ounces of scotch later, we tipped the tired waitress and walked down to my motel room. Altogether, I'd spent about thirty-five dollars of my short stake on a cage and a golden bird to put into it. But that was what a stake was for.

3

Not really hoping, I'd left the room inspection-neat, with just the bedside light on. She stood, looking around, and then sat down in the desk chair and crossed her graceful legs. She slapped at her knee with the soft gauntlets, held in her right hand. 'You might offer a lady a cigarette.'

'And a drink. I've got a bottle of Cutty Sark here.'

'Ah, that's what I was missing in those highballs. Liquor.'

There were five or six diminished cubes of ice in the pitcher; I spent most of them on her drink, saving the rest in case she needed another one. I was being the very efficient seducer.

She sipped the drink in short, quick swallows, puffing on the cigarette furiously. 'What do I do now?'

'You might try taking your hat off.'

'For a starter?' But she stood up and

went to the mirror, swung the wide-brimmed hat off hair that was shinier black than I'd expected, and poked at her hair with her fingertips. I sat down on the edge of the bed, feeling as nervous as she acted.

But I had a reason; six and a half years' worth of reason. I couldn't figure hers; I surely hadn't drawn the only beautiful twenty-five-year-old virgin in the country.

Looking at me in the mirror, her back still to me, she said: 'You might at least kiss a lady.'

I had my hands on her shoulders before she'd finished the last syllable and was turning her around. She came against me all in a rush, her lips opening under mine, her body pushing harder against me than I was against her.

My hands were busy rediscovering what they'd never forgotten. But then, human, I had to breathe, and she was saying, 'Please, just a minute. My dress.'

When I let her go, she made no effort to go into the bathroom or to turn her back on me. She just bent over and grabbed the hem of her frock and pulled it over her head. Then her slip followed it, and she stood, staring at me, proud and frightened, all at once. Her bra and panties were of the finest cloth, silk or nylon I suppose, but they were no smoother than the lovely skin that showed in long, smooth bands above the stockings and below the bra.

'Do you — do you want me to take my stockings and garters off, or do they — do they excite you?'

It's an old adage that a man has no conscience at a moment like that, and it should have been especially true after my long period of chastity, but I said: 'What the hell are you scared of, Colomba?' And when I said it I knew perfectly well that it was going to ruin everything.

'It's only because it's — I hate clichés.'

'You hate clichés, but it's the first time you ever did anything like this.'

She nodded, her eyes wide.

'Have you left your husband, are you planning to leave your husband, or are you just getting even with him for something?'

She looked the question. I bent over,

24

picked up her hand, and kissed the pale line the ring had made around her finger.

She said, 'I don't know. I'm on my way to a lawyer . . . You don't care about that. I'd better put on my dress and go, as the woman said.'

'Have another drink.'

Colomba said, 'Shush,' and tilted her head, listening. 'I can still hear music up front. It's not too late to pickup that hostess, or the waitress.'

Editing somewhat, I said, 'I wouldn't pinch either of their tails with a pair of borrowed fingers.'

She laughed at that. It wasn't much of a laugh, but it did. Counting like a little child, she bent down three fingers, one at a time. 'I'll take another cigarette, and then another drink, and then another kiss . . . Want me to put my clothes back on?'

'Hell, no.'

Now I didn't mind at all if she did, or if she didn't. I told myself I'd even sleep with her, hold her in my arms all night, and not make a pass. Probably I wouldn't have been able to do that, but it's what I told myself.

A motel room on a freeway is a hell of a place to fall in love. A married gal in her underwear is a hell of a thing to fall in love with. An ex-con on his way to turn a trick is a hell of a lover — but that's the way it was.

And I didn't have to test my over-tortured body more than an hour after she said she'd take the drink, the smoke and the kiss. When she was ready, when she was over being frightened, it went off fine.

Just fine.

Once in the night she woke up and said, 'Do you have to be anyplace tomorrow?' and I told her not till Monday. She said, 'Me, neither,' and went back to sleep.

That was Friday night. All day Saturday, and all Sunday, and this night and two more. We'd have ourselves a time.

Saturday night, as it is supposed to be, was the best of all, though it was not like any Saturday night I, or maybe any man, had ever spent. We'd had a long lunch with cocktails and wine, and French food

26

and handholding, and a lot of looking into each other's eyes. And then we'd come back to the motel and made love, not sex — but love as I understood it, long and gentle and wonderful. Afterwards, I'd fallen asleep; and when I woke up, I was ready to reach for her again, but I didn't. There was something else I had to do first.

Colomba was lying on the bed, eyes half-closed, lips pulled back in a faint smile. I said, 'I'm going out for a while.'

Her eyes opened wide, watching me.

'About two hours,' I said. 'Get some sleep. We're going to do a full-sized job of town-painting tonight. With champagne.'

She said dreamily, 'I don't like champagne very much.'

'Well, neither do I, but that damned silver bucket on the table does something for me.' *And so do you*, I thought. *Oh, what you do for me.* But I had this little trip to the outside world that I had to make.

She said, 'We'll have champagne on the table, and then we won't drink it.'

'That's the highest type of high life.'

Her eyes closed completely. I was quiet getting dressed and getting out of there.

I knew where I had to go; a small downtown hotel. The guys in the house had mentioned it. I wasn't going there because I hoped for something better. This wasn't for pleasure, but for a test, for something I had to know.

An hour later, I knew. The lobby of that joint, the cocktail lounge, and the mezzanine were full of them: the classiest call jobs in the business. There were blondes and brunettes and redheads; no brown hairs, though. Come to think it over, I've never seen a woman on the call who had brown hair; they all bleach it or dye it deep black.

I talked to a couple; I bought drinks for a blonde. But nothing happened. My blood didn't pump any faster, my skin didn't sweat, my hands didn't feel like reaching. So I drove back to the motel, and it was all I could do not to break the speed limit and buy me a mess of cops.

But Colomba was still there and still on the bed, and the minute I saw her, I was as ready as I had been when I left her.

She smiled and said, 'We'll pour the champagne on the potted ferns, huh?' And to me it was the cleverest thing anybody had ever said.

4

Monday morning, there being no justice in the world, I woke up feeling fine: no hangover, no aches, no pains. Colomba was still asleep; the Venetian blinds were drawn. When I went into the bathroom, I peered out, and gusts of water were walking across the empty lot behind the motel. The sky was the color of a prison guard's soul.

I showered and shaved, and put on a pair of clean shorts; we'd shopped for me on Saturday. Colomba was no woman for asking questions; she hadn't shown the slightest curiosity about a man who didn't own a damn thing but a car and a bankroll. Which bankroll, I thought with a dropping stomach, was pushing down towards a hundred measly dollars.

When I came back into the room, she was propped up in bed with the Sunday paper we'd bought and never gotten further than the comics with. She looked up. 'Very becoming, Larry.'

My name was still Lawrence Rankin.

The shorts had polka dots, blue ones on a white background. I strutted in them, and she laughed. Then she said, 'What time's your date?'

'Eleven o'clock. I could come back here later and — '

She shook her head. 'No. This is it, and I think you know it. And . . . ' She looked down at the paper. 'And I want to thank you. Nobody was ever nicer to anybody.'

'What do you think you were to me?'

'Larry, you were so damned decent that first evening, when I was acting like a ninny and a milksop and a — oh darn it, I'm going to cry.' She slipped out of bed and vanished into the bathroom. She'd been sleeping raw.

That was a nice final picture to take away with me. I felt the way she did; I didn't want a bleary, teary farewell. In our two mornings together I'd learned she was no fireman when it came to dressing; she liked to come out of the bathroom with everything done, from shoes to her naturally shiny hair.

So I dressed slowly, packed the bag she'd bought with me, and went on out to the car. My car, looking like a poor relative alongside hers. I drove out of the motel, and turned towards downtown.

There was a little shopping district a mile in town from the motel. An old-fashioned jeweler's clock said it was only ten-fifteen. On impulse, I turned in.

She'd said once she was a Virgo, and I'd make a joke, of course, and she'd said that that was the sign of people born in late August, and they were always very neat.

The jeweler, rather surprisingly, was a lady, young and animated. She said that the birthstone for August was sardonyx, and showed me a pair of earrings, very handsome, but not gaudy; thirty bucks, sales and federal tax, the sort of thing that Colomba's husband would never question.

The earrings flashed as the jeweler held them up, and she kept turning her hand to show me how slim and neat her fingers were, how bright her fingernails. I looked further. Her dress was low-cut, and she was leaning over so I could appreciate it. But I didn't. She could have been wearing a prison guard's blue serge for all she did to me.

I said I'd take the earrings, but it wasn't that easy. She said I ought to be sure, and screwed them on her own ears, walked up and down the narrow aisle of the store for me, trying to let me know that she had a nice figure and well-shaped legs. But she got no more response from me than the call women had, and my heart rose. It was not just my awful bodily need that had driven me to Colomba; it was more and much more, more than a man can hope to find in a lifetime. And now I was driving myself frantic to get back to the motel before she checked out.

This dame was telling me it was her husband's store, but he had gone over to a Father's Day meeting at the school. He'd be back in an hour, and then she'd have nothing to do but go home to her apartment and sit. She lived at —

The address went in one ear and out the other. I cut my lips thin and said, 'You want to sell those earrings or keep them?'

She took my money quickly enough then, and I was loose, cutting back along the freeway, making the proper cloverleafs and crossovers and under- and over-passes.

The big car was gone. The key to our room was in the lock, as per the request of the management for checkers-out, but the maid hadn't gone in yet. I did.

No trace of her, except you always think you can smell a little perfume when they are gone. Probably, though, it's the combined odor of all the females who have ever used that room.

No trace of love or kindness or humanity, except a rumpled bed and a little steam on the bathroom mirror, and the unfolded Sunday paper she'd read while I showered. I don't read papers, myself.

I started out, and then turned back. Something had been torn out of the paper. A picture, it seemed like, from its position in the story. The story: 'Bank Officer Who Stole Quarter Million Turned Loose.'

She hadn't torn out the story; just the

picture. That told me a lot. She didn't care what I'd done or where I was going. She'd just wanted a picture of me.

Maybe she'd just taken the newspaper photograph because it had looked like me, not because she'd thought it was me. But that was a crazy idea. She knew now who I was — a crook, and a crook on the road to pick up a crooked two and a half hundred thousand dollars.

The floor of the motel room was concrete. The gift box crushed under my feet nicely. I picked up what was left of the wreckage and put it in the wastepaper basket because there was no use making trouble for the maid; there's enough trouble in the world already. And I had my share of it: buying the earrings had brought me nosing near the seventy-five-dollar fence, where the suckers lived.

5

At five minutes of eleven, I entered the Union Station and walked, neither too fast nor too slow, to the neon sign saying 'restaurant.' Jerry Quarry was at a table four rows from the door; close enough to make a quick getaway, far enough so he didn't get the double-0 from everybody coming in. Jerry was a pro, from his too-narrow hat brim to his too-pointy shoes.

I sat down facing him and said, 'For God's sake take your hat off.'

'This is a railroad station. I wanta look like a traveler.'

But he took it off and held it out in front of him. 'Nifty, no? You getting plenty, Danny?'

There was a necessity to go along with Jerry, to talk his language, to share his interest. 'I'm fighting them off, boy.'

It was a convict's answer, a quick one to protect the only privacy you have left when they hand you that prison denim: the secrecy inside your head. But Jerry Quarry was my friend, and Jerry Quarry was hep. If anybody could help me find Colomba again, he could. And I wanted to tell him about her. Still, I kept my mouth shut. She was something, someone, too good to talk about with the Jerry Quarrys of the world, even if they were my friends. I would use my head. I would make some money, and use that to find her. With dough you can do anything, and Jerry Quarry was going to help me make dough.

'I know,' Jerry was saying. 'The dames, they can smell out a guy who's been away and is all full of eager. It wears off after a while. You ready to go?'

'Ready as I'll ever be, soon as you tell me a little about the deal. I don't walk into anything blind.'

Jerry turned to the waitress standing behind him and said, 'Two coffees and doughnuts.'

'Yes, sir,' the woman said. 'Two doughnuts apiece?'

'Sure, two doughnuts. You think we're cheap?'

'Sugared, plain, jelly or chocolate?'

'For Gawd's sakes,' Jerry said, 'you gotta give your life history to get the edge taken off your hunger in this joint? Bring us one of each kind of doughnut you got, two coffees, and don't hurry, on account of people get fallen arches from hurrying.'

'My goodness,' the waitress said and walked away, twitching her hips.

Jerry said, 'Never pass up a waitress. If she's had a bad lay, at least she can bring you some scoff at night.'

I was back to where I'd been a few days before. The weekend with Colomba — some weekend, from Friday night to Monday morning — and the casual contacts with motel clerks, car salesmen, and gas station people had gotten my talk almost back to where it was before. Just before.

'You're pretty famous,' Jerry said. 'Yesterday, coming back from setting up the trick, your picture was in every paper on the train. The guy who snatched a quarter million and lost it on a bus.'

The guy, I thought, who found true love, and threw it away on a weekend party. Jerry's eyes were swiveling every minute as this blonde and that brunette and the other redhead went by. They all looked like trash to me.

A long life of celibacy stretched ahead of me; a thought that made me laugh. I knew myself better than that. But it seemed like a long life of second best. There wouldn't be many more chances like the one I'd thrown away.

But I had to answer Jerry. He'd been talking about the stories about me. 'I never read papers,' I said. 'They're full of lies. They ache me.'

Jerry's eyebrows crawled towards his hair, and he grinned a little. 'You don't read papers, huh? Even when they're about yourself?'

I shrugged all that off. 'When do we turn this trick?' I asked. 'I'm nearly flat.'

Jerry shook his head. Some sort of male perfume floated out from him. 'Wait till the twist blows,' he said, not moving his lips. I knew, of course, he meant that I should wait till the hash-slinger was farther away.

So I waited, and was treated to an educational study of courtship among the lower animals. The waitress — she was two inches too big in the hips, but she compensated by being two inches too small around the bust — put all four doughnuts in front of Jerry, and leaned on his shoulder while doing it. She said, 'Our doughnuts are the best in town.'

This was something I wouldn't have known how to answer, but Jerry did. Slowly turning his head, he took a long, leisurely look down the front of her uniform. 'That's the truth,' he said. 'I never saw doughnuts I liked better.'

He'd moved slowly, but she was almost slothlike taking her weight off his shoulder. 'You ought to try the jellied ones,' she said. 'Jelly makes 'em just right.'

'That I'll do,' Jerry said. 'That I'll do. This afternoon.'

'Be sure and get in before four,' the waitress said. 'By five minutes past, I'm at the bus stop, on my way home.'

Then she waggled her hips to where a middle-aged guy had been tapping a coin impatiently on the counter.

Jerry was my meal ticket. I laughed and said, 'What a worker!'

Jerry nodded complacently. 'Yeah. Too bad, but we're gonna be rolling by four.'

'Working?'

'Yeah,' Jerry said. 'Maybe. If you'll do for the trick. It's a short con, but it's got some heavy in it, and you never been on the heavy, have you?'

'No,' I said. 'You know it. I'm a one-time loser, and that for embezzlement.'

'We're working with two other guys.' Jerry filled his mouth with doughnut and washed it empty with coffee, and went on, 'Don't tell them what you took the fall for. The boys don't like embezzlers. An embezzler, now, he has double-crossed his own outfit. But I like you, Danny. You're a right guy. You smelled okay to me the first time I glimmed you, up there. It's not like you was a pimp or a pickpocket. Them guys is strictly no good.'

'Thanks.'

Jerry waved his hand; such praise was nothing to him, and he was glad to give it to me. 'So, all right. It's a liquor dealer we're knocking over, a crook, and all you gotta do is tell him the tale. I bought the setup from the boys who'll do the heavy.'

'This is in town here?' Nothing he was saying made me wildly excited about the trick, but I had to make a living. When I'd pulled my first trick, I'd told myself I wouldn't go near the quarter of a million for three years after getting out of the pen. Interest in me would die down by then, and I could open my cache without anybody looking over my shoulder, ready to clobber me and take the money. Afterwards, I'd go to some foreign country and live high and long and happy. I had it all figured out. In three years I could select my country; no use doing that ahead of time. There'd be plenty of places that wouldn't extradite a man with all that scratch.

Oh, sure, I had it all figured out, except one thing. And in that respect, I was like nearly every man in the penitentiary.

They had all planned perfect crimes, with one flaw apiece. One flaw, one prison term.

Mine never occurred to me till I was nearly out. How was I going to support myself for those three years? All I knew was how to be a bank teller and how to run a prison library. The first was certainly closed to me, and the second unprofitable . . .

So here I went, supporting my big crime with little crimes, and well aware I walked a frayed tightrope. But my big binge, my weekend with Colomba, was over. This little trick with Jerry, and I'd go someplace cheap, the foothills of the Ozarks or a beach on the Gulf Coast and live on nothing a week till I was forgotten. Maybe I'd even do some light day-labor. Painting boats or driving a bus or a taxi. I'd go without drinking, without a woman, until the time came to get my money and go abroad.

Jerry was talking. 'Let's blow,' he said. 'There's a train at eleven fifty-eight.'

'I've got a car,' I said.

He looked around as though I'd said a

bad word. But nobody had heard me. 'Hot?' he asked.

'No. Strictly legal. Bought and paid for.'

He shook his head. People who bought cars were out of his social circle. Upstate, Jerry had seemed a fine fellow, a cut above the other cons; now I was beginning to realize I'd fallen in with a cheap crook, a hustler of the lowest order. I was sure that first-class con men and bank robbers and so on did not steal cars: that was a punk's trick. It occurred to me to wonder what Colomba would say if she saw me with Jerry. Life was going to be different if I saw everything through her eyes from now on. I was very glad I hadn't told Jerry about her.

Jerry looked sly now, and said, 'The guys are already there. They went down on the bus. This car, now, it ain't in your own name, is it? All that stuff in the papers about you.'

'The car isn't in my own name.'

He said, 'Yeah, sure, you're a brain . . . So you got car-buying kind of dough, Danny?'

'I've got less than a hundred bucks to throw around; you don't get far on that these days.'

'Ain't it the truth?'

I found a half inch of cold coffee in the bottom of my cup and drank it. I didn't like the way Jerry was looking at me. Perhaps I was a fool, but it hadn't occurred to me till then that maybe there was no trick to turn, except one on me. Jerry and I had been buddies up in the house, till his release a year ago. He wasn't a squealer, a stool pigeon for a big mob, or any of the other categories of prisoners whom I avoided. A right guy. But he could read, and he could listen to prison gossip, and a quarter of a million dollars gets itself talked about. He could be leading me to a place where he thought I could be made to talk about the money.

But, in just a couple of days of freedom, I'd run through almost all of two thousand dollars. I needed a stake, and Jerry was my only chance.

I said, 'We ought to get moving.'

Jerry said, 'Yeah, yeah. Sooner we start,

sooner we cop.' He shoved away from the table, picking up the check. 'I'll maybe make it back here soon.' He made a fifty-cent piece ring on the black glass table top.

The noise was a bell bringing the waitress. 'Well thanks, big shot,' she said, and rubbed her big hip against Jerry's in passing.

Jerry said, 'You was right, best dough-nuts in town,' and slapped quickly and furtively at her rump. She giggled, and we left her for the cashier. Jerry paid with a dollar bill, scooped up his change and pocketed it without counting.

He was helping himself to a toothpick when something changed in his face. He dropped his eyes and walked without looking up till we were out in the main waiting room. 'Railroad bull,' he said through his non-moving lips.

I lowered my own head. It wasn't hard to walk that way; all you had to do was head towards the stronger light of the front door. What do they call flowers when they follow the light? There didn't seem to be much point in asking Jerry.

Outside, Jerry looked up at the bright sky and said, 'They give me the creeps. Railroad bulls, hotel dicks, the guys that watch for shoplifters in department stores, traffic cops — all of 'em. They can spot us, Danny; and me, I never did a thing in my life to hurt a department store or a railroad. But they got a down on us.'

'We're on the other side,' I said, to be saying something. 'My car's over here.'

But Jerry wasn't listening. He was furious at something, at nothing, at the whole world. 'How do they spot us? I don't look nothing like you. Not a single feature the same! You take Whitey Barber, up at the house. Do you look like him? Do I? We're people, not a bunch of horses.'

The lonesome cry of a human being for recognition as an individual. I said, 'We're as conspicuous here as a couple of sea lions in the desert. Let's get in my car, or someplace.'

Jerry grinned suddenly. 'Old Danny. Both-feet-on-the-ground Danny. Sorry I blowed off.'

47

'Think nothing of it. Here's my car.' There was still better than an hour left on the meter; I hoped whoever got the space would be someone to whom a dime mattered.

But Jerry looked at the meter head. 'Ten cents an hour, three hours for two bits. Wonder what time they clean these slots out? Guys could come in here with overalls on, screwdrivers and such on their belts, and make a killing.'

Sudden irritation made my stomach burn. 'We're not off on any penny-ante deal like that, are we?'

Jerry shook his head and climbed into the car. 'Naw, naw. This is a triple-barrel deal, Danny. A one-two short con tonight, and that gives us a bankroll for a big con. You'll see. You'll like my boys, too. Heavies, but nice guys. Truth is, they never had it so good as they will now, with a smoothie like you to front for them. Turn right here, and follow the freeway till there's a crossover south.'

I put the car out into the stream of traffic and headed out of town. I was aware almost at once that we'd headed straight for the motel that had been my and Colomba's headquarters for the long weekend. I smiled, sentimentally returning to the scene of passion to get a glimpse of the building where I'd enjoyed myself, like a schoolboy going a block out of his way to pass his best woman's house.

'Danny.' Jerry's voice was quiet, almost sad. 'It's none of my business, but tell me something. That fall you took, the one I met you on — that was your first one, wasn't it?'

I knew what was coming. 'Yes, it was.'

'It was my third,' he said slowly. 'And likewise with the two heavies we're gonna make a meet with. In a lot of states, including the one we gotta work in, it's four times and out. For life. The fall for life.'

'I know, Jerry.'

He was very quiet as we went along the divided highway. There was the motel, and tonight someone else would be checking into the room Colomba and I had had. I hoped they would have as good a time as I had had.

Finally Jerry said, 'It's like a ball game. I use to play a lot of ball when I was a kid, and was on my high school team. Shortstop, and I batted better than .300 . . . I was on the team my first fall, but the second time, a goddamned harness bull got me in the ribs with a .38, and I never been able to throw good again.'

The melancholy tones were ruining the day. I said, 'What's like a ball game, Jerry?'

'A guy's up at bat, and a ball comes at him, zingo, wowie. So he knows it's gonna be a strike, but he lets it go; it isn't just right for him, he'd maybe pop fly an' out, or maybe get a one-bagger. He waits. But when there's two strikes and three balls on him, he hits at anything that he can reach. He knows that, and the pitcher knows it. It's like us, like me, with three falls. I'll go for anything. And if the corner gets tight, Danny, I'll go the gun route, because I'd rather be blowed up than put away for good 'n' all.'

'You're telling me to pull out, Jerry. But if I don't go your route, as you say, what happens to me?'

'The way I read it, you got considerable scratch someplace.'

There it was again. Did they want me for the front Jerry talked about, or because they thought — they knew — I had that quarter of a million put away? I said carefully, 'If I knew where that money was, it would be too hot to get to for two or three years at the least. In the meantime, I have to eat. Think any bank would take me back? Think I could be a librarian because I worked in the library at the house?' I swung into the right lane. 'This our turnoff?'

'Yeah.' Jerry looked out at the thick, fast traffic and shook his head. 'You drive good, Danny. So you're in with us. I gotta say I'm glad. You're a front, but you're a brain, too. Me, I'm a simple heist guy, and the other two, they're even simpler. With you along, we'll make it good.'

The car finished a cloverleaf and we headed south. I asked how far we were going. Jerry cleared his throat. 'Over two more state lines, but these are pint-sized states. This part of the U.S. of A. is thick with these little cities. Not New York or

Chi, but cities nevertheless.'

But he said never-the-less, making three words of it, proud of speaking in such a fancy way. He'd been to high school. I asked, 'When do I get to know what the trick is?'

'The big con we make up later, with you as the brain,' he answered. He stretched in the seat, belched, and lowered his window to rest his elbow on it. 'It's a two-man bank, father and son, and we're gonna big-con the son. But tonight, ah, that's a nice one. There's a town down here ahead — maybe you heard of it? Cedar Brakes?'

The car almost went off the road; my foot did come off the accelerator, and cars honked at me. I drifted over into the right-hand lane where I could go slow. 'Good God, Jerry! If it's the only Cedar Brakes I ever heard of, that's a federal town, a government installation. Tight as a Methodist on a convention, with a high fence around.'

'Keep on driving; you're holding up all these good people. Why, that is correct, Danny boy. Except that three years ago, while you was takin' a vacation, they opened the gates in that there fence, allowing us citizens to come and go at our will.'

I was looking for a crossover to turn back. Though back meant no more to me than forward; I had no home.

'Sorry, Jerry, but I'm not sitting in on a heist in a town where a phone call can close the only way out.'

'Ways out,' Jerry said. 'There are two gates. But this ain't a heist. If it was, why cut a guy like you in? This is a short con, and the mark can't beef.'

Maybe I'd better explain. There are two kinds of cons, short and big. In the short con you take the mark for what he has in his pocket; in the big con you send him for more. There had been plenty of con men in the house; I'd heard them talk. They were particularly the kind to use the library, though I got the impression they were studying to work out new cons when they were released. But they were nice guys, a very jolly crew.

Incidentally, the victim of a heist is a sucker, but the victim of a con is always a mark. My late housemates were very particular about such points. Mark, like my first name.

'Supposing it is a con,' I said. 'How do we get away if the mark squeals?'

Jerry began to laugh. 'This mark won't squeal,' he said. 'He's a lousy thief . . . '

This had to hold me for a while. Jerry was still chuckling when traffic, unaccountably, started to slow down. I slowed with it, worried a little.

There was a sign to slow down, and then another sign, 'All Cars Stop,' and then a third one, 'State Officers Ahead.' I stepped on the brakes, and Jerry stopped his laughter, all at once. 'U-turn here,' he yelped. 'Let's get outa here.'

'Shut up.' Suddenly I was cool and almost happy. 'It's probably just a license check, drunk driver inspection. Keep your head down, pretend to be asleep if you want to. They don't care about anybody but the driver.'

'Oh, God!' Jerry huddled down in the seat. 'How I hate those cops. All cops, everywhere.'

'Sure, sure.' Ahead of us the line of cars

had huddled together, barely moving. I dropped my gear shift into the low slot, and let the car edge along, but after a moment I had to throw in the clutch and stop altogether.

'Why don't they snap it up?' Jerry asked. 'They think people got nothing to do but hang around, waiting for a bunch of lousy cops?'

'Shut up, Jerry. Just take it easy.'

The car ahead pulled out and went down the highway at a decorous thirty miles an hour, the gait adopted by all drivers who have just been spoken to by a policeman. I coasted in to stop with my elbow even with the belt buckle of an enormously tall state trooper. In the background, two other troopers and a man in the khaki of a deputy sheriff stood watching, their thumbs in their gun belts.

'Driver's license, please.' The cop had to bend nearly double to talk; it seemed strange that one of the shorter men hadn't taken the duty.

I handed it over, together with my proof of ownership of the car. I didn't look over at Jerry, who was pretending to be asleep in a masterpiece of bad acting.

The officer handed back the license. 'For the next twenty miles,' he said, 'don't stop for any hitchhikers. Two women ran away from the state reformatory.'

'Okay.'

The officer started to wave us on, then dropped his hand. 'Your friend all right, Mr. Rankin?'

The name had come off the license, of course. I had almost forgotten I was Lawrence Rankin, but I recovered and said, 'Sure. He drove first, then I took over.'

The cop nodded, and this time finished the wave.

Jerry didn't straighten up, but his eyes popped open. 'Oh, boy,' he said. 'Dames! Keep a sharp lookout, Danny. We can scoop 'em up, hide 'em in the trunk. That'll make everything hunky — '

The bite in my voice surprised me. 'If we see them, we keep right on going,' I said. 'Are you going to pull a con or go on a bat?'

He didn't answer for a mile or two. The car hummed, its speed regained. Then he said, 'Danny, you can get too hard-nosed. It's all right, you're a brain and a front, but you can get too much all one way.'

I didn't bother to answer him. We came to another cloverleaf, and I slowed till Jerry said, 'Left. We're going to Altonsburg.'

Shortly after the cloverleaf, traffic slowed down and bunched up again, and then there was a state trooper waving us to get along, not to stop and rubberneck at two women being hauled into a state car by deputies and troopers. The women were just a flash in passing, but I got an impression of stringy hair and pinched faces and gaunt, ungainly bodies.

'Okay,' Jerry said. 'Okay, Danny boy. We're going to work.'

6

Nobody in the filling stations, restaurants, or bars that we stopped at was anyone Jerry wanted to impress. I paid all the tabs from the Union Station to the bottle club in Altonsburg, where we met the heavies. The half a hundred in my wallet didn't weigh me down.

A bottle club, because this state had a twelve o'clock closing law, and it was after midnight when we pulled in. Two hours back along the freeway, Jerry had phoned from one of those booths that stand along express roads these days, looking like they ought to be up on the corner of a pen wall.

The heavies had a bottle; Jerry, the big shot again, ordered setups, tipping the droop-eyed waiter with a dollar bill. One of the heavies, named Chester, said, 'You can scoff here.'

'We et along the road,' Jerry said. He waved a hand at me, a farmer taking his prize calf to the state fair. 'Whatta ya think of Danny here?'

The other heavy was named Grif; he wore a worn-out business suit over a gray flannel shirt. 'Looks like a legit to me.'

'What else?' Jerry said. 'You think Chester could pull this deal, with that mug of his?' He poured drinks into the setups.

Chester's rib cage was deep and wide under a horse-hide jacket. When he grinned, he showed a lot of gold; his snuffling breathing indicated a past involved with a canvas ring. 'He looks good to me, Jerry, if he's on the up and up. You on the up and up, Danny?'

'Sure,' I said. 'Sundays, when I'm not running the police department, I preach in a Holy Roller church.'

This killed Chester. A wheeze was born somewhere around his twisted fingers, traveled up his muscle-bound arms, and burst out of his store-bought teeth. 'Hey,' he cried with delight, 'this guy's all right, Jerry. Whataya do Saturday night, Danny?'

'Sing in the synagogue.'

Grif didn't like this. 'Hey,' he said, 'what ya got against Jewish people? I celled with a Jewish fella onct. He was the nicest guy I ever knew.'

Jerry rapped his knuckles on the table. 'This gets us nowhere. It's too late tonight to make the con; how's it for tomorrow?'

'Sooner the better,' Grif said. 'The truck's hot.'

Jerry slapped the table with the palm of his hand. 'I told you. I even give you dough for a truck.'

Chester dropped his little eyes. 'We got hot. We got hot, and here was these women — not hookers, Jerry, real nice women — and the next thing you know . . . ' He shrugged, very unhappy.

My liquor was dead in a dead stomach. These were what I had to work with; these, without a break, were what I would have to live with till it was safe to go for my quarter of a million.

They were what might be framing me for that same quarter of a million.

Grif said, 'But we done good on a warehouse to keep the trucks in like you said, Jerry. It's crost the tracks, no windows, nobody's been near it for years.'

'Dirt street?' I asked. 'Or paved?'

'Dirt,' Grif said. He stared, wondering what I was getting at.

'Oh, fine,' I said. 'Nobody's been near it for years, and now you've put truck tracks right up to it. Maybe by now, the cops are right there.'

'Oh, golly . . . ' Grif said.

Jerry snatched up the bottle. 'On your way, lugs, now. Get old boxes, newspapers, something. Wipe out them tracks.'

They left. They were scared of Jerry. Big as they were, dumb as they were, this man frightened them. There was more to Jerry than I'd seen in the house upstate, than had shown in the day we'd been together in the free world. I studied him, looking for that thing; and, as so often happens when you look for something in this world, I found something else.

Jerry was looking at me, and he was afraid of me. Or had respect for me. The two things looked alike to a guy who'd seldom read either in anyone's eyes.

'You're a brain, Danny,' he said. 'We'da

blowed the whole con if you hadn't thought of the tracks to that warehouse. A real brain.'

Which told me a lot. Before, I had been a front for him and his two heavies. A front, and a mark. But now, I was really in.

'Tell me about the con,' I said.

'First let me buy you a drink.' He called the waiter and ordered setups and cannibal sandwiches. He poured, holding the bottle high, making a sort of ceremony of it. Then the waiter was gone, the toast was drunk, and Jerry was serious. 'It's like this,' he said. 'There are three liquor stores in Cedar Brakes. On gov'ment concession. Means they pay no rent; instead they pay the gov'ment company that runs the town a percentage of everything they make. You get it?'

'No,' I said truthfully.

'Two of the liquor dealers are crooks,' Jerry Quarry said. 'With all that dough they make, they gotta do it the crooked way.' He shook his head at the perfidy of mankind. 'They been buying liquor where the gov'ment doesn't know about it, so's it won't show on the books, so they don't have to pay percentage. You get it?'

I got it.

'The boys, Grif and Chester, they got hold of a truckload of that hooch. The crooked hooch from out of state.' He was Mr. Prim now, very proud of not being that kind of crook. 'They get in touch with me, they want me to sell it back to the guy they hijacked it from. He can't squawk, see?'

I saw.

'So I was going to do it, but I'm not a front guy. When you called in, I knew we had it made.'

There was no doubt about it; it was a nice setup. The liquor dealer wouldn't squawk; he'd know that if he had us arrested, we'd tell where we got the liquor. There were serial numbers on tax stamps; he wouldn't want to call attention to the stolen bottles. I only had one question.

'Why did the boys have to steal a separate truck? Why not keep the truck the liquor was on?'

Jerry Quarry's voice was sad. 'It was an army truck. A real fed job. One of the officers at Cedar Brakes, he's a crook.' I had never seen anyone look more superior. 'There's army trucks going in and out of Cedar Brakes all day'n night. Food for the soldier boys there, ammunition, I don't know what all. We're not dumb enough to latch onto an army truck and keep it.'

The truck driver and the army officer — probably a sergeant — would never mention that their load had been hijacked, since they weren't supposed to have a load. They'd be too glad to get the truck itself back.

'It's a nice setup, Jerry,' I admitted. 'Let's take the rest of this bottle and find a hotel room. Tomorrow's our day.'

But there was still the night to get through. The wound of separation from Colomba was still raw; someday it would heal, of course. Till then, I fought the temptation to buy an extra bottle and liquor myself to sleep.

* * *

I was Harry Webster, attorney-at-law when I stopped at the liquor store in Cedar Brakes. Lawrence Rankin sold the car to Harry Webster, and the boys knew a printer in the city whose past insured a shut mouth. He used quick-drying ink on Counselor Webster's business cards. The good counselor had a Peoria address; everyone knows Peoria is big in the whiskey trade. I paid for the work with almost the last of my stake.

The name of the liquor concession store was the Good Cheer Shop. The name of the owner was not Mr. G. Cheer, however, but Mr. Nelson Hill.

He turned over my card to see if there was anything on the back; there wasn't. I said, 'I'm down here investigating a truckload of stolen liquor for one of my clients.'

Mr. Hill's eyebrows climbed an eighth of an inch. If his eyes changed expression, I couldn't see it, but I've seldom seen eyes that do change. He said, 'You'd better come up to my office.' Somehow I got the impression he'd bought stolen liquor before and was afraid that I was looking for some of it. It was a very good impression for him to have.

His office was a half-floor, sort of a mezzanine, hung above the store proper. Most of the mezzanine was used for wine storage, but the office was a box up towards the front, with a window through which he could watch the three clerks dealing out Good Cheer down below.

When we came in, an ash-blonde was using the peep window, sitting relaxed in an overstuffed chair, a cigarette in her hand. Mr. Hill introduced us; his wife. Mrs. Hill at once drifted out of the office, and Mr. Hill took her place, though there was a desk for him to sit behind. This call of mine might be important, but it didn't justify letting one of the clerks pocket a dime.

I took the other side chair and left the desk to the angels. We lit cigarettes. Mr. Hill said, 'Drink, Mr. Webster?'

'No, thanks. I thought it was illegal to open a bottle in a package store?'

Mr. Hill shrugged cheerfully. 'I'm not opening a bar in my office. Just having a snort with a friend. A new friend. I make friends easy, Mr. Webster.'

'So do I,' I said. I pulled an ashtray nearer me and licked my cigarette.

That made him pick up the ball. 'You represent an insurance company?'

'No. If I did, my problem would be easier.'

Mr. Hill looked a cheerful inquiry. The guy was as smooth as the contents of his best bottle.

'You see,' I said, and then hesitated. 'Well . . . ' No use overdoing it. 'This is confidential, isn't it, Mr. Hill?'

He tried to look like the finest confidant in the world.

'You see,' I picked it up again, 'the trouble is, I found the load.'

He leaned forward, forgetting to watch his clerks. I hoped each of them pocketed a ten-spot. 'The stolen load of liquor? I hadn't heard of any load disappearing. The wholesale salesmen gossip like old women.'

'This wasn't taken from this state. But I found it near here . . . You don't care where. And now I don't know what to do. My client's insurance company has already paid off. And you know the trouble you have, getting a consignment of stamped liquor back on the tracks in fair-trade territory.'

He nodded. He knew indeed. Liquor, and anything else that is fair-traded, has to go through channels. Each time it passes a distributor, a wholesaler, a retailer, it has to be marked up. Also, it accumulates tax stamps — federal, state, municipal — like a rolling stone does not accumulate moss.

'I'd like to close this truckload out,' I said. 'At half price and pocket the loss, for my client. Anything we get back, the insurance company will be glad to get, so long as they don't have to know how it happened.'

He turned back to watch through the spy window. He couldn't have been more indifferent. 'Sure,' he said over his shoulder, 'if your client and their insurance company got a quarter back, it would be more profitable than loading and reloading through channels.'

He had said quarter price. I had said half price. We were in business.

'Thirty-three and a third on the dollar should make everyone happy.'

He let me have the left eye, while his clerks got the right. 'It should.'

'For a quick deal. Today.'

Mr. Hill said, 'Tonight. My clerks leave at nine-thirty. Closing time is nine, in this government town. You'll be with the truck?'

'I'll be on the truck — with two strong men to do the unloading. Cash, of course.'

He gave it the grin it deserved; it was impossible to think of him writing a check on a deal like this. He stood up, and we touched hands without really shaking. At that moment his wife drifted back into the room, taking up her post at the spy hole again. She must have been tin-earing us; maybe she had some of her own money in her husband's business, and was checking up to see he didn't give it to anyone. A charming couple . . .

Half of them, the male half, were on hand when Grif piloted the stolen truck to the back door of the Good Cheer that night at ten. I'd given Mr. Hill a half-hour to get greedy in. He opened the steel door for us, and I got down; Chester followed me to guide the tailgate up to the loading dock.

Nelson Hill had the state liquor catalogue in his hand. As each case slid off, he looked up its price, called it to me, and I divided by three. When there were two cases left, we had passed sixteen hundred dollars; four hundred apiece for Chester, Grif, Jerry and me. Nice.

Grif slid the last cases backward; Chester got them onto the platform. Mr. Hill peered at them. He frowned and fumbled through the catalogue. 'Not here. I never heard of this stuff. It must be a direct import.'

I looked too, though I knew what I was going to see. I said, 'Argentine brandy, for God's sake.'

Chester was a slightly better actor than Grif; I'd tried them both. He said, 'Hey, boss, can Chuck'n me have that, if you don't want it?'

'Sixty bucks a case, wholesale, on the inventory,' I said. 'Hell, no.'

Mr. Hill's face got the rigidity with

which he hid eagerness. 'That would be twenty dollars a case on our deal,' he said. 'No, I couldn't pay that much; an unusual item like that is liable to sit on my shelves for years.'

'Forget it,' I said. 'Leave it on the truck, boys. There's a young lady of my acquaintance who used to live in the Argentine; she'll think I got it especially for her. Let's go upstairs and settle this thing — and I'll take that drink you offered me today.'

Nelson Hill was staring at the two cases of Argentine brandy. Of course he knew what they were. This order had originally been meant for him, but he couldn't admit that; it was illegal to buy liquor from a wholesaler outside his state. He said, 'You know, in a town like this, we have every kind of screwball, from all over the world. Experts on the atom and rocketry. Maybe I could move that brandy.'

'Forget it,' I said again. 'It probably tastes so horrible you'd lose a customer.'

'I'll tell you what,' he said. 'I'll buy one bottle, and we'll try it out. A deal?'

He was in the trap I'd set when I first saw the off-beat brandy. He had a customer for it, or he wouldn't have ordered it; and the retail price was something like ninety dollars a case. On two cases he'd make a hundred and forty dollars' profit, and for that amount of money, Mr. Hill would have sold Mrs. Hill's ash-blonde scalp.

'Forty dollars is forty dollars,' I said. 'For my client, of course.'

'Of course, for your client.'

'A deal. One bottle, at two dollars.'

He started to dicker me down the few cents that the bottle should have been and then thought better. The boys lit cigarettes and climbed into the truck cab, and Mr. Hill and I climbed to his perch above the darkened liquor store.

I'd been afraid the ash-blonde would be there, but she wasn't. He got glasses out of a cupboard; nice glasses that he'd gotten free, from the brand name on the side. 'How'll you take yours?'

'Straight,' I said. 'If you can't drink a brandy straight, you oughtn't to drink it.'

'I see you know your liquor.' He

poured, then pushed a glass to me.

'Let's finish our business first,' I said. 'I make it seventeen hundred and eight dollars.'

He nodded, divided the sum on his tally board, and said, 'Close enough.'

Close enough, hell! It was right on the nose: seventeen hundred and eight dollars and thirty-three cents. I'd let him have the thirty-three cents, big-hearted me. After all, my end of the deal was a four-way split; I was giving away less than a dime of my own money. Any time I can be a big shot for less than a dime, I leap at it.

He reached inside his gabardine coat and took out a long, flat wallet. He held it under the desk and counted out bills, then finally slid them across to me. I counted them, said, 'Check,' and started coughing. So I took out my nice clean handkerchief from my breast pocket; I didn't want to cough in a customer's face.

When I finished my coughing, I put the money in my pocket with my left hand, and picked up the brandy glass with the same hand. 'Skoal.'

'Skoal,' he said, and knocked that Argentine brandy down in two swallows.

But me, I had one terrible cough; my brandy went into my nice, clean, oversized handkerchief. I'd bought it that day for that very purpose.

'Not bad,' he said. 'Not bad at all. No cognac, but interesting.'

'It has a rash, impudent taste to it,' I said. 'And the not-too-rare aroma of horse manure.'

He said, 'Huh?' and neither laughed nor frowned. His breathing was getting deep and regular, and he was going bye-bye, as anyone will who has just drunk the approximate ounce and a half of chloral hydrate that had been in his two ounces of brandy. Seventy percent chloral hydrate is the old-fashioned knockout drops of the Bowery. Both my heavies knew how to make it if we hadn't been able to buy it, but we'd gone far enough south so you could buy all kinds of soothing syrups in the drugstores. Down there, the religious old grandmas need something to take the place of the liquor that they wouldn't touch for fear of hellfire.

As he went away to lullaby land, I counted the money he'd given me. That's right, it was a hundred bucks short. So I took his wallet out of his pocket and emptied it. He had been ready to pay up to three grand, which gave me pause. Since it was his truckload originally, he should have known what was on it. Had Chester and Grif double-crossed Jerry and me? Or had Mr. Nelson Hill gotten confused? Had he had so many orders out, he wasn't sure which hijacking we were returning to him? Or had he short-changed me in the count?

I decided it was the latter, and emptied the wallet into my pocket. Then I strolled downstairs and told the boys to get the cases back on the truck, which was unnecessary because they were nearly done. Jerry had said that two of the liquor dealers in Cedar Brakes were crooks; and, not wanting to waste my gasoline — a national natural resource — I had gone and seen Mr. O. K. Beverages on the same trip that had introduced me to Mr. Good Cheer. So now we drove over there, maybe too cheerfully, because Grif kept leaning on a bottle of the Argentine brandy.

Our new mark was waiting on his loading dock. He was named something like Keyser. He gave me twenty-four hundred dollars for everything but the open case of Argentine brandy, which I kept for a souvenir of Mr. Nelson Hill. Keyser wasn't the chiseler that Mr. Hill was; he'd offered a higher percentage of the wholesale price, so we let him keep the liquor.

Anyway, the boys and Jerry were all agreed that the third liquor dealer was no goniff and would probably have hollered copper — federal copper — if we'd tried to do business with him. So the O. K. Liquor Store had the stolen hooch on its shelves, where the sight of it would probably give Mr. and Mrs. Nelson Hill heartburn, once his soothing syrup had worn off.

We drove away from the liquor store, with Grif burping; unloading those heavy cases on top of the Argentine brandy had upset him. But now it was my time to relax with a couple of swallows of Perla de la Plata. I tried to sing, but I couldn't think of anything but Columbia the Gem of the Ocean, which was appropriate enough for a government town, but not for the occasion.

Grif decided to settle his stomach with some Perla, and it did wonders for him.

Chester said, 'That first mark's sure gonna be sore.'

'He's a jerk,' Grif said. 'Hope he isn't the kind of jerk who's a big man around the police station.'

'That's a happy thought,' Chester said.

It was. Nelson Hill had looked like an unfriendly customer. But he couldn't squeak; all he could do was take it and like it. Maybe it would teach him that honesty was the best policy.

7

Those heavies were stupid, but they knew their business. We drove a wide circle getting back to the city from Cedar Brakes; we dropped Grif off in a small town, and went back into the scrawny hills. Chester took a dirt road that ran above a washed-out gully, and when he thought the time was right, he had me get out. Then, standing on the running board, he put the truck into low and let her get going, and stepped off. She crashed to the bottom of the gully.

While I watched, fascinated, Chester took a bottle out from under his coat. It looked like it held a medical laboratory exhibit, but when he pulled it out, I saw it was just clothesline that had been soaking in kerosene. He tied a stone to one end of the clothesline and flipped it down to the truck; then he stood there, grinning, before he knelt to wipe all traces of coal oil off his hands. Finally, he lit a cigarette

78

and used the rest of the match to start flame running down the clothesline.

As we strolled casually down the dirt road, he laughed. 'Let the square johns figger that one out,' he said. 'She'll blow up in about twenty minutes.'

Five of those twenty were gone when we reached the paving at the foot of the gully road. Grif was just pulling up with a shiny little two-door sedan as we finished our stroll. He drove us to where we'd left my car at the bus terminal parking lot in the city and fed a municipal meter a quarter.

'That's a nice little bus,' he said, patting the stolen two-door. 'The guy had her broken in gentle.' Then we got in my car, and I took them to the cheap hotel they were staying at, and drove back to where Jerry Quarry and I had a room.

The desk clerk was dozing as I went by him; he half-straightened up, and then recognizing me, collapsed again. I had hardly put my hand on the doorknob when Jerry opened the door and pulled me in. He put his free hand to his lips, and I nodded.

He crossed to the bathroom, went in and started the tub running, then beckoned me in after him. Over the roaring of the water, he whispered, 'I never trust a hotel with built-in radios. This tima night, the clerk's got nothin' to do but tin-ear us. It go all right?'

'A touch over fifty-four hundred.'

'Fifty-four lovely cases. Boy, oh boy, are we hot!' But he had done nothing but put the heavies in touch with me. 'Cut up four ways, and how much is fifty-four hun'nerd?'

I stared at him. But working as a teacher and a librarian while I was a con, I had learned how few of these lads — even the ones with slick manners — had finished grade school. Jerry had said he was a high-school lad, but the truth wasn't in Jerry. 'Thirteen-fifty apiece, Jerry.'

'Boy, oh boy.' He wet his lips. 'We really oughta split three ways — one for you, one for me, one for the boys together. They're just backs without brains.'

And in talking to them, no doubt, I was just a guy who'd done a little spieling;

why give me a full cut? But I smiled and said, 'Three-fifty apiece, and four grand for operating expenses, Jerry.'

He was a kid whose lollipop had been pulled out of his lips; a teenager who'd just been denied the family car. 'We could — '

'We could grow up. We're going on a big con. Things like that need capital, they need front, they need a bankroll. If we don't snatch those things now, we'll be going from one short con to another till we slip and go back to the house.'

'We can't go back. You can, but Chester and Grif and me, we can't.'

'Okay, then.' The bathtub was almost full. I reached down and turned off the cold-water tap. The hot water made enough noise to keep our voices from reaching the radio in the bedroom, though it seemed improbable anyone was still listening. 'Thanks for the valet service. My good man, I shall recommend you highly as a tub-drawer.' And I turned off the hot water.

Jerry grinned, but it wasn't a happy grin. If he could distinguish between

Frankenstein and his monster, he might have compared himself to the former just then.

Dawn was beginning to light the bathroom window; I hadn't been to bed for twenty-one hours. The hot water unkinked muscles I hadn't known were tired. I lay back against the porcelain and relaxed.

We had a smooth-working group. We were, as Jerry had said, hot. I didn't know what his big con was, but whatever it was, we could manage it. My brains, Jerry Quarry's endless energy, Grif and Chester's muscles. But we'd taken too many risks on the liquor trick. Slick as the burning of the truck had been, it had been foolish to use a stolen track to begin with. You can buy a good second-hand truck for six or seven hundred bucks, and there's no danger of someone recognizing it on a highway. And the knockout drops, the chloral hydrate, had been crude. There was a simpler method of taking a man out, if only I could think of it. A woman who offers to cheat on his wife with him? A guilty mark is a quiet mark.

But a dame meant a five-way cut instead of a four. Unless the dame belonged to one of us, and was willing to share her man's take? That didn't seem likely . . .

By a very natural process, my thoughts had gotten back to Colomba, the perfect companion for me. We'd shot what? About two hundred dollars in the course of our protracted weekend. Now I had three hundred and fifty to spend, if my plan was adopted by Jerry and the boys, as it was sure to be. I was entitled to a few days off, after the trick I'd pulled. Time to blow, say, two hundred dollars — in a motel, with Colomba.

But I didn't know her last name; I didn't even know what city she lived in. She'd been on the highway when I met her. I didn't even know whether the lawyer she was going to consult was in the city where'd we'd caroused. Probably not, or she wouldn't have been so open about going to nightclubs and restaurants and so on with me.

A hundred and eighty million people in the United States, and my chances of meeting this particular one again was one in a hundred and eighty million. Which was no chance at all. I'd been so damned sure she was just a weekend thing, I hadn't even bothered to look at her license plates.

The water was getting chilly. I got out of it, rubbed myself warm with a couple of bath towels, and went out into the bedroom. Jerry Quarry was asleep. I pulled down the shades against the growing day, got into the other twin bed, and stretched out. We were to meet the boys at the bottle club at three. In the meantime, I held the stakes.

Not that they trusted my honesty; their faith was in my good sense. If I had tried to skip, Chester and Grif would have caught up with me and worked me over. That I didn't need.

8

My pocket happy with almost forty-two hundred fat clams, we moved south and a little west to celebrate the Good Cheer trick. There was more or less legal gambling in the resort we went to, and this my three comrades embraced with enthusiasm. That was something I hadn't known — the universal craze for betting among the criminal element. It leaves me cold, all of it, from craps to roulette. But the boys couldn't even sleep till what they had in their pockets was gone.

Me, I ate big meals, delicate ones with four or five courses to them. I went to little night clubs in that resort town and heard the kind of music that never came over the house earphones in my cell. I swam a little in a heated pool.

But I never picked up a woman. Bought a drink for one or two in the little jazz boites, but never went through a door with one — and I knew it was because I'd gotten Colomba into my blood. I'd hit the jackpot my first try out of the house, and it had ruined sex for me.

So I daydreamed. When the time came to move for my quarter of a million, it would be a cinch. A man with that kind of dough could hire the biggest detective agency in the world — Burns, Pinkerton, whatever — and find a woman with a wild first name. Could do it from Belize or Tunisia or wherever, and have my darling wrapped up and delivered to me there.

Thinking this way, it was only natural that I could cut the time I'd pledged myself from three to two years. In two years I could move on my cache, get my two and a half hundred grand . . .

★ ★ ★

The second night there, I came into our hotel room at two-thirty in the morning, and there was Jerry Quarry. He had his coat and tie off and his collar was open, his eyes red and his hair wild.

86

'How come you're not listening to the click of the little ivory ball, pal?'

'You're not funny, punk.' He blinked his red eyes at me, swung his hands together hard. 'They cleaned me. Red, sixteen times in a row.'

'And you were on black?'

'Whatya think, punk?'

'That's the second time you've called me that.'

Jerry had been perched, apish, on the edge of the bed. He got up now. I had never noticed how wide his shoulders were before. He came at me, hunched over, swinging his arms against each other. 'And you are. Fresh fish! Full of how Mr. Big you are, 'cause you've pulled two tricks!'

'What's eating you, Jerry?'

'Dough. Simple old dough! If I'd a had my grand that you held out on me, I coulda gone on! How long you think a wheel can show red?'

If I'd said what came into my mind — that the wheel would show red enough times to break him and not one more — he'd have killed me. Instead I said, 'All right, Jerry. Let's move on. The big con.'

'Gimme my money, punk!'

'I can't. I haven't got it.'

This brought him out of it, where a slap in the face or a cold bath wouldn't have. He sat down again. His voice was hoarse, almost a whisper. 'If you've blowed our dough . . . '

'I haven't blown it. Where are the boys?'

He shrugged. 'They got in a crap game. They was cleaned out two hours ago; the guys who cleaned them are setting 'em up to a big feed.'

Grif and Chester were simpler men than Jerry Quarry. Simpler, and maybe smarter, though it would have surprised them to hear me say so. They didn't gamble to win; they gambled to be gambling, and, broke, had no regrets.

'We're ready to go, then. The money — four thousand dollars — is in a short-term treasury note.'

He had calmed down. 'Wha's that, papa?' he asked.

'It's a piece of paper the government gives you in exchange for using your money for ninety days or so. You get a little interest.'

Jerry shook his head. 'What the hell do we want with anything like that?'

He should have gotten it at once. But I explained, 'The mark's a banker, you said. So, okay. We — I — take him this note and ask to borrow on it. He makes a little money. It puts him in a good mood.'

Jerry wasn't completely stupid. 'Yeah, yeah. And small-time grifters don't drift around with that kind of paper in their pockets. It's class.' His face was falling back into its natural lines again; this was as exciting as roulette to him. 'You're a brain, Danny, a real brain.'

'Named Scott Read,' I said. 'The brain is named Mr. Scott Read.'

He laughed, standing up and moving to the bathroom. 'You sold yourself the car again?'

'Right.'

'Man, man,' he said through the water he was dashing on his face. 'That poor little car isn't going to know what to call you by now.' He came out, threw his towel on the floor, reached to the bureau, and pulled out a fresh shirt. 'We can roll tonight. I know where the boys are.'

'Let's sleep,' I said. 'I want to get to the mark fresh.'

He stared, belligerent again. Then, unexpectedly, he laughed. 'Okay. Hell, while we sleep, our little old piece of paper's making money for us, right?'

'About a penny an hour.'

'More than anybody ever paid me for sleeping before.'

So we slept . . .

I was alone when I — Mr. Scott Read — drove the car into Altonsburg. Jerry was coming in on a train, to take a room at the only decent hotel in town. He'd reserve one for me, too, his big-shot boss. The boys were on a bus behind me; they'd be looking for jobs. Grif, it turned out, was a good sheet-metal man, though he'd learned his trade in a pen, stamping out car licenses, or something like that. Chester was just a roustabout, but his strong back usually got him a job at once. The boys didn't mind working, so long as they could look forward to not working.

Altonsburg was not much of a town; its

population hovered around the twenty thousand mark. But it served a rich and varied farm country, and there were two big factories in the county and another one in the town itself. Altogether, about fifty thousand people did what the economists call their 'primary purchasing' in Altonsburg; and if they wanted to do any banking, they could use either the First National or the Union State Bank.

Jerry Quarry's mark was in the Union State Bank. Physically, the bank was a handsome little structure; the front was slightly taller than square, built of blue sandstone and architecturally contrived with memories of a Greek temple. The cornerstone was of red sandstone and announced that the structure had been built in 1870, Darrel Oxford, president. High, narrow windows broke the front; they were covered with bronze grillwork, more for decoration than for protection. The glass behind the grillwork was laced with the gold leaf of a burglar alarm.

Inside, the floor was terrazzo, with brass dividers. Light from the high windows reflected off the brass and the specks of metal in the terrazzo. The light also fell on the pale, high forehead of Raleigh Oxford, whose glass cubicle stated that he was the incumbent president of the Union State Bank. Looking at Mr. Oxford, I wasn't sure how many generations separated him from the founder. Approximately ninety years had passed since Darrel Oxford accepted the keys from the architect and — no doubt — made a speech inaugurating this building.

Raleigh Oxford was not ninety, but he was surely past seventy. And the cashier over there — cashier and vice president — was his son, Jerome Oxford; and not a young man, either, for all that he seemed to regard his titles as honorary and his duties as those of a bead bookkeeper.

Mr. Bookkeeper sat at a wooden desk, in advance of a middle-aged lady at a metal desk. Both of them had comptometers or adding machines in front of them, and both seemed to be posting accounts. Two women of thirty or more stood behind teller's windows, while a man of fifty wore a guard's uniform and sat at a desk marked 'Safe Deposit'.

And that was the Union State Bank. It wasn't much, but it smelled of money.

Mr. Oxford was talking to me. 'If you're not overfond of night life and excitement,' the old man was saying, 'you'll like Altonsburg, Mr. Read.'

Mr. Read — me — looked skeptical. Mr. Oxford wasn't my mark; it was Junior we were after. But a long conversation with Senior was like money in the wallet to me — the quickest, easiest way of impressing Junior.

Jerry Quarry was rude and dangerous and thoroughly unfit to be the companion of an elegant guy like me. But he knew how to set up a mark. Jerome Oxford was in his late forties; he had graduated from a college and from a good school of finance, and then he had come back here and planted his rump on a swivel chair and waited for his father to use all that fancy education. But his father never had. For all the good he did the bank, Jerome could have taken the commercial course at high school and quit. He ran the comptometer; he maybe was allowed to buy the janitor's supplies, and he said 'Yes, sir,' to his father. He was ready to blow like the house's steam whistle in an escape. And when he blew, we were hoping he'd spray money all over us.

'We've got a little country club here,' Old Man Oxford told me. 'Only nine holes, but grass greens!' I didn't know what other kind of greens there could be. 'The Altonsburg House has fine food, and if you get tired of that, the Eagle Inn on the edge of town has a chef direct from Paris, France.'

It was nice to know the chef hadn't lingered on the way. But I was here on business. 'Mr. Oxford,' I said, 'I'm looking for a bank with discretion.'

His white eyebrows crawled towards his gray hair. He had more hair, though it was grayer, than his son did. 'That is why we are a state bank,' Mr. Oxford said. 'Small services, and special ones, are our stock in trade.'

'Well, dandy.' I reached in my inside pocket and pulled out my ninety-day government note. 'I want to borrow on this.'

He took it and looked it over. He couldn't find anything wrong with it, because there wasn't anything wrong. He said it: 'Good as cash, Mr. Read.'

The Mr. Scott Read that I was being just then nodded. 'Sure. Also, it draws a little interest, which cash doesn't. I don't want to lose that interest, but it happens I'm going to need that money for about two weeks. If I cash it, I lose ninety days; if I borrow on it at five percent, I'm quite a bit ahead.'

The old gentleman said, 'I am sorry. But our rate on short terms is six percent.'

Proper indignation suited my role. 'With government paper for collateral?'

'Bookkeeping, you know. Processing. Overheads.' He waved his hand at his expensive battery of accountants: his son and the middle-aged lady. The son was goggling hard at us, and trying not to be seen doing it. If caught, I suppose his father wouldn't let him have dessert with his lunch.

I was biting my lip, trying to make a decision. I said, 'There's the First

National, of course,' and watched Mr. Oxford get just a little nervous. 'But I don't want to start out with them if I'm not going to keep on, and they are big, and every employee extra means one more mouth that can talk.'

'Well put, Mr. Read.'

'Fifteen days, three thousand dollars, five and a half percent.'

He looked at me. My firm, round tones were still ringing in his ears. He said, 'Done, Mr. Read.'

And so he was. From that moment on, his bank was as good as looted. I nodded, and he raised his hand and called, 'Mr. Jerome!' not loud, but clear. Never before in my life had I heard a father call his son Mister.

His bookkeeper son scuttled from behind his desk and came towards us. Seen close up, he looked more in his late thirties — which Jerry Quarry said he was — than in his fifties, which was what he'd looked behind his desk. His father told him what kind of papers to make out, in great detail, though the deal was one that any twenty-year-old kid would know how to inscribe after a month in the bank.

Mr. Bookkeeper went away again. He walked as though his shoes were too tight for him; maybe he had to wear his father's old ones.

While the son did his piddling chores, the father tried to pump me. 'I gather, then, that you're thinking of settling in Altonsburg, Mr. Read.'

None of this was any of his business. I let him make what he could out of a smile, and then I said, 'If everything goes right, Mr. Oxford, I'll be a client of your bank's a long, long time.'

'You're in business for yourself.'

This got him a steely glance. None of his business.

He flushed a little and said, 'A fine county. If you need labor — and what business doesn't? — our population is docile, native-born. Fine, hard-working people.'

'That I wondered about,' I said. I waved at the front window. 'The name of your bank, I mean.'

Mr. Oxford puffed a bit at that. 'Mr. Read,' he said, 'my grandfather founded this bank! He served in the Union army!

The name meant something very different in those days, before Mr. John L. Lewis and Mr. Walter Reuther dragged it down into the mire.'

It was kind of fascinating. I said, 'I just wondered,' and sat back while he huffed himself out. So now he knew this about me: I carried four-grand notes in my pocket, and I planned on hiring enough help to worry about union conditions. Things were going fine. I booted them along a little. 'Mr. Oxford, which real estate agent in town would you recommend?'

This hit the jackpot. He shook his head regretfully. 'Oh, I couldn't answer that. You see, five of the town's leading realtors are clients of ours; I couldn't show favoritism. A banker walks a pretty tight rope!' He laughed unconvincingly.

'A list of the five will do me fine. It will be assurance that my business doesn't get run through that gossip mill over at the First National.'

'Now, now, Mr. Read. I didn't say that the First National employees are indiscreet. But a little bank like this . . . ' He waved a hand to indicate what a jewel and a gem a little bank was. Junior was shuffling towards us. His boss and father took the papers from him, looked them over quickly, and laid them in front of me. The pen he offered was fat and substantial; its red and black rubber and its gold tip gleamed as handsomely as when the pen was new, thirty years before.

But Mr. Scott Read was a business-man. I read the forms — as a matter of fact, they were identical with the ones the bank had used back before I took my fall — before signing. The last paper to be signed was the check for three thousand dollars. I endorsed it and said, 'Might as well put this in a checking account for me.'

Oxford Senior beamed. Oxford Junior scurried. I wrote a check for a hundred, and Junior ran to cash it. His father kept me busy in light conversation. 'This, we like to think, is the most close-mouthed bank in the world.'

I looked to where the triangle on the son's desk said plainly: 'Mr. Jerome

Oxford, Cashier.' I asked, 'Mr. Jerome's your nephew?'

'No,' the bank president said. 'He is my son. Hurry with Mr. Read's money, Mr. Jerome!'

'Yes, sir,' Junior said.

9

Jerry Quarry was waiting for me in the lobby of the Alton House. He was very deferent to me as we walked back out to my car and watched the bellboy get my bags out. I gave the boy a dollar to take my bags up to the room Jerry had reserved for me, and we took off in the car.

'We just spent a thousand bucks,' I said. I handed Jerry all the papers I had gotten in the bank: the note, the checkbook, the list of realtors, the Chamber of Commerce map of the county.

'How come?' he asked.

'Borrowed three grand on our four-grand government note. Chances are, when we come to leave town, we'll be too busy to redeem the paper.'

'I sure'n hell hope you know what you're doing.'

'I sure'n hell do. I've got an invite to the mark's house for dinner. His old man just about ordered him to lay out the red carpet for me.'

Jerry Quarry's sulkiness lifted a little. 'He tell him to lay down his wife? I heard the mark's old lady's a nifty quiff.'

'Too bad,' I said, thinking of Colomba. 'I was halfway planning on getting a broad in to work on the mark, if he acted slow. But if he's got it good at home . . . '

'Better if we don't have to cut in a dame,' Jerry said.

'Oh, sure. This looks like a good place.'

I parked the car and we got out. Jerry lifted a little trowel and a waterproof cardboard box out of the backseat. We got out and walked around the vacant field for a while.

Once upon a time this had been good farm land, but it was farmed out. Real careful, hard-working farmers had ploughed it and harrowed it and done everything else to it that real, conscientious farmers can do, and wind and rain had done the rest: this was pure clay and wouldn't grow a damned thing. Fifty-cents-an-acre land.

Jerry dug up a trowelful of dirt and put

it in the cardboard container. I consulted the maps we'd gotten for the con: Washington maps, maps from the state capital, maps from colleges. Then I wrote something on the lid of the box; some crap that didn't mean anything, and the location of the field, in legal terms, section, range and township.

The country was flat; nobody could see us, it seemed, though you can't be too sure. This had to be strictly on the up-and-up, a legitimate promotion.

All this had been laid out before I got on the job. Jerry Quarry had once worked out a fall in the tile plant of a pen; you can learn anything in a house. He'd had this mark spotted, this deal laid out, long before the two heavies came to him with the short con of the liquor deal. Then I'd come along, and he was ready to roll.

We stopped at six more places and added six more samples to our supply. Then we drove back to the hotel and took our samples upstairs.

Jerry's room was next to mine, but, of course, it wasn't as big as mine. I was the big shot, the front.

There were no built-in radios in this Alton House. Jerry unplugged the table radio and said, 'What now?'

I patted the box of clay samples. 'You checked in like I said?'

'Like we agreed,' he corrected me. 'Hell, Danny, this is my con. You talk like I was hired help.'

He was dangerous, and the heavies would go his way. It was necessary to keep him happy. 'Just getting in the mood for the meet with the mark,' I said.

But he was still a little sullen. 'Sure. I started to write Ohio Ceramic etcetera after my name in the hotel book, caught myself, and scratched it out. But hell, Danny, we don't got to do none of this. This mark ain't congenial; he won't chum up with hotel clerks and such.'

'No, but his father's got everybody in town where it hurts. He'll get the information, and he'll let sonny-boy see it. He treats Jerome Oxford like a piece of furniture; an adding machine, you know.'

'Yeah, I knew.' He giggled, suddenly, a terrible sound coming from his calloused throat. 'Ain't it a beauty, Danny?'

'A beauty,' I said, and took off my shirt and went into the bathroom to shave while Jerry moved to the phone, ordered double martinis for each of us, and sat down again, lighting a cigarette and humming little snatches of a song as he waited. Just before room service arrived, he remembered, and plugged in the radio again.

We drank, and I finished dressing myself up to banking-circle standards. Jerry was to fix the clay samples so it would look as if we'd been working with them, and then go make a meet with the heavy boys. We had worked it out that the meet would be in the third place listed in the local classified directory as a bar. All I had to do was look at the street map in the back of the phone book and follow it to the mark's house.

It turned out to be what you'd expect: a three-story Victorian house, mansarded, jigsawed, shingled. There was a broad porch to cross, and then there was a modern electric bell to push, and then there was a fanlight to stand under till someone opened the door. And, after a few seconds, someone did.

Colomba.

Colomba of the remembered, unmatched, unmatchable Friday-night-to-Monday-morning weekend.

It was Colomba, and then again, it wasn't. The features were the same — the big eyes, the firm lips, the delicately chiseled nose. All the same. But the figure was different. Colomba had walked the earth proudly. This lady proceeded with an apologetic slump. Even her hair had lost its bright shine. And her eyes had become just something for her to see with.

She was very good. When she saw me, her eyes widened, and her nostrils tightened, and that was all. She smiled, and the smile was hardly ghastly at all. Someone like Mr. Jerome, who was not used to smiles, might have taken it for a real one. She said, 'You must be Mr. Read.'

'Scott Read, And you must be Mrs. Jerome.'

'Mrs. Oxford,' she said. 'Won't you come in?'

I followed her well-remembered hips into the house, down a long, wide hall, and turned right into a small back parlor. Parlor, not living room or drawing room; an old-fashioned parlor with stiff-backed, overstuffed furniture and a fireplace with — for God's sakes — artificial logs in it. The table lamps looked like they had been converted from kerosene — what else were the big hollow glass bases for? — and there was a chandelier on which blue parrots were uncomfortable in front of red and green fields, strangely fenced with lead strips.

Jerome Oxford stood up in his thin, pale way and said vaguely, 'Mr. Read, good of you to come. I thought we might have some sherry before dinner?'

I nodded and took the seat his hand waved at.

Mr. Jerome said: 'Susan, if you'll get the glasses, I'll go for the sherry.' He pulled a ring of keys out of his pocket — evidently the sherry was precious — and shambled out of the room.

Colomba was already gone. She got back first, carrying three cut glasses on a

107

tray that probably came from the World's Fair of 1896. I said softly, 'Susan?'

Some color came into her cheeks, certainly a novelty in that house. 'My middle name,' she said.

I continued to stare at her.

Her nostrils flared. 'Don't you know anything? All little women hate their names. They change them, they make up new ones. I made up Colomba when I was in grade school. I used to make my friends call me that. It means dove, or pigeon.'

'I thought it meant gem of the ocean.'

Her lips thinned and paled. 'And you? You told me your name was Larry something-or-other. Now it's Scott Read. But it's really Mark Daniels, isn't it?'

There were footsteps in the hall. The mark — old Mr. Bookkeeper, Mr. Householder, Mr. Jerome-of-the-Bank — was about to show. I said quickly and harshly, 'My real name is I-love-Colomba-till-I-die,' and took two steps away from her gasping face and turned to meet Mr. Jerome.

Mr. Jerome came back, carrying the

bottle on the tray. It was half full, and it had a label that said it was sherry. The label also said that it was the finest California sherry, so fine it had been given a name: Fruit of the Vine. Full, it had probably cost seventy cents.

I didn't dare look at Colomba. I'd dealt her a foul blow, saying what I'd said when she didn't have time to recover; but I shouldn't have worried. Women handle that sort of thing without flinching, from the time they're three years old, or maybe two.

She said, 'Let's sit down, shall we, Mr. Read?'

She sat down and I sat down, but her husband continued to stand, shifting from foot to foot, waving the bottle. 'There's nothing like a little something before dinner, Mr. Read? Susan?'

There was a lot more difficulty in thinking of her as Susan than there was in remembering what my own name was. I said, 'Fine, fine.'

Colomba said, 'If you think so, Jerome.' She whispered, 'How in the world did you find me?'

'How does the salmon find the right stream to swim up?'

'Oh God, Larry, don't make love to me. That's all over.' She was close to crying. 'I couldn't stand it. Not in this house.'

The last thing I wanted was to make Colomba cry. The next to the last thing, maybe. Maybe the last thing was to blow the con. I said, 'I'll behave, kid,' and she smiled, and folded her hands in her lap, and was a good housewife again.

He offered a glass to me, took one himself, and left Colomba to shift as she would. 'Your health,' he said, and raised the glass and then lowered it again. He stared anxiously at the bottle. 'Perhaps I'd better lock it away.'

Colomba had apparently been through this before. 'Your father never goes out at night,' she said. 'And anyway, he'd smell it on your breath.'

Mr. Jerome sighed and nodded. 'Yes, I suppose he would. But you're right, he doesn't go out after dark.' He turned to me. 'Forgive us, but in our family, we're all concerned about Mr. Oxford, my

110

father. It simply isn't good for him, at his age, to get excited.'

I was staring down into the yellowish-brown pool of Fruit of the Vine. It probably wouldn't kill me, but it didn't look or smell like something that would add years to my life expectancy. I stalled. 'Your father doesn't approve of drinking?'

'A banker should be in full possession of his faculties, day and night.'

'Sounds like a rich, full life.'

That was an error. His head went back, and whatever blood he had rushed into his cheeks. He shot a quick look at Colomba, but she wasn't laughing at him. 'Well, your health,' he said, and we drank.

Fruit of the Vine tasted every bit as bad as it smelled and looked. Mr. Nelson Hill of Good Cheer would have been ashamed to handle it. Well, maybe Mr. Hill was not up to being ashamed of anything, but it would have been bad business. Good merchants don't poison customers.

Colomba seemed to be used to the stuff. Hell, I'd wasted a lot of money on her, feeding her Cutty Sark and Old Fitzgerald. She didn't gasp a bit before she said, 'Dinner's ready, when you are.'

Mr. Jerome stood up. 'Unless you'd like another, Mr. Read?'

Mr. Read — me — waved the thought away with a flick of his graceful wrist.

My host went ahead of us down the hall. He pulled aside an oil painting of a stag or a deer or an elk or something — I'm no outdoors type — revealing a cabinet he unlocked. He put in the bottle. As Colomba and I passed him, I glanced in. The Fruit of the Vine jug was his whole wine cellar. He was right: that stuff should be kept locked up. Nobody wants burglars writhing on the living room floor, having to have their stomachs pumped at two in the morning. That's no way for a decent householder to live.

We sat down under another stained-glass chandelier in an old-fashioned dining room, at a table covered with a heavy linen tablecloth that had been nicely darned here and there. I passed up a chance to praise Colomba's needle-work, and a sharp-nosed maid started bringing plates of soup through a swinging door.

The time had come to go to work. Looking down at my plate, I said, 'Very unusual porcelain, Mrs. Oxford.'

My eyes were right on her, but no ex-con needs to look at something to see it. Her husband was coming to life.

He said, 'You're not in the chinaware business, are you, Mr. Read?'

Crafty old me. I told the mark, 'Not exactly.'

'I made this set of dishes,' he said.

My name became Mr. Astonished. 'No! Why, man, they're superb work. You're wasting your time in that bank.' I took my knife and gently tapped the edge of my soup dish. 'But this isn't local clay. Pacific white, isn't it?'

Jerome Oxford, now completely alive, now a full man, nodded. 'That's right. When I was in college, I spent one summer vacation at Laguna Beach.' He pushed his soup away. 'I hardly ever get a chance to talk to a ceramist. I don't imagine there's anyone in the whole county tonight who ever heard of Pacific Coast white, except you and me.'

'If your work was this good when you

113

were college age,' I said, 'I certainly am going to enjoy seeing what you're doing now.' I bent my head and ate my soup like a little man, though it wasn't very good soup; sort of chickenoid.

There was a lot of silence, broken only by the clinking of my spoon on the plate. Neither Colomba — Susan Oxford — nor her husband was eating. I let the silence build until I could look up and frown.

Jerome Oxford's face was red. 'Banking takes up all my time,' he said. 'I never went on with my ceramics.'

I stared. I looked down at my soup plate. Susan Oxford rang a little dinner bell, and the maid came and took our soup away and started bringing in a leg of lamb and the dinner plates from the set. Finally, I threw the hook into him. 'Forgive me, Mr. Oxford,' I said. 'I don't mean to be rude. The bank is your family's and all that, but it's still a pretty small bank. And you have no idea how rare competent industrial ceramists are. By that, of course, I mean people who can make porcelain, and who have executive backgrounds as well.'

Susan Oxford said, 'You sound like you're offering Jerome a job.'

Now was my time to be Mr. Confused. I couldn't manage a blush, but such things as fidgets, collar-pulling, and the down-casting of eyes were a cinch for me. Under cover of all this, Jerome Oxford carved me some overdone lamb — or mutton, it was so dried out I couldn't tell — and added some deceased peas and a charred bit of potato or so. The maid brought it to me.

Finally, I said, 'No, not at all. My business here has nothing to do with ceramics.'

They looked like they didn't believe me.

We had finished our bread pudding and were choking on our de-caffeinized coffee when Jerome Oxford said hesitatingly, 'I built a gas kiln once. In the cellar. But Fa — but I never had time to use it. If you — I mean, while you're here in Altonsburg, I'd like you to feel welcome to it.'

That was a terrible temptation. Colomba was still alive, somewhere inside Susan

Oxford. And I was being given an open, legitimate reason to call on her at any time — hell, to take her down into the cellar with me.

But the big con didn't work that way. I declined the invitation, protesting — too often for conviction, of course — that my interest in ceramics was absolutely amateur, and at ten o'clock I got out of there. At that, I'll bet the sharp-nosed maid reported to the bank president that sonny-boy was roistering far into the night, rendering him unfit for his bookkeeping duties the next day.

I drove around town till I found an all-night diner, and bought myself a bowl of chili. Not that I had to get the taste of the Oxford cooking out of my mouth. It hadn't had any taste.

10

We built our con slowly and with loving care. It took three weeks. Fortunately, I didn't have to eat at the mark's house again; I imagine that his wife, the ex-Colomba, put her foot down, and refused to invite me. I know I asked them to dinner at the hotel, and Mr. Jerome — I called him that now — showed up alone, and made polite noises excusing her. I don't remember whether she had a headache or a case of galloping leprosy.

After I'd been there a week, and after Jerry and I had mailed two packages of clay samples and three letters to the biggest ceramic factory in the country — the letters said we were sending them the samples and would be glad to act as their agents in buying clay beds for them — we got a letter back. Of course, it said that they had ample clay deposits and were not considering building any branch plants, but thanked us for our cooperation and kind offers, regretfully, yours sincerely.

That didn't matter. We had expected to be turned down; we'd have been damned embarrassed if we hadn't been, because we'd suddenly be legitimate. But what mattered was that the letter was thumbed over. I didn't worry about it being read; the kind of hicks we were working would be scared of a post-office rap.

We were in. Natch, we'd had the hotel bellboys take all our packages to the post office for us, and we'd bought stamps for our letters at the hotel desk so the clerk could see to whom the letters were addressed; but we couldn't be sure that the hotel staff were stooges of the Oxfords and their banks. Now we knew.

'It's a pretty setup,' Jerry Quarry said. 'It's a natural.'

'You know,' I said, 'I've never asked you, but how did you get onto it? Did you buy it from somebody? It's almost too good — a county with clay deposits, a banker who wishes he was a ceramist.'

Jerry looked proud. 'I didn't buy

nothing from nobody. I made it up. I been nursing it for years. Like this. I told you, I worked in the tile-pipe plant in this house. So the free man who was head of the tile works, he wanted to train us boys. He was always buying magazines and books like, for us to read. And in this magazine there were some pictures of plates and cups and so on, made by this man that the magazine said was now vice president of a bank.'

'I see.'

Jerry Quarry grinned. 'All my life I been on the heavy. Holdup man, second story — but of course, if it's a one-story house, we work it, too — I been lookout for a coupla Johnson brothers, you know, safecrackers — and I wanted to come up in life a little. And when I met you up at that house, I said here's my front at last. And we're going to make it.'

'Sure,' I said. 'We're going to make it.'

'It's even in the right place. Any kind of hitch, there's a mouthpiece two counties away licensed to work in this state, ready to jump in, though he doesn't know it. A real mouthpiece, Tom Atchison.'

People who don't know anything are always calling lawyers mouthpieces. People like reporters, which is one reason why I gave up reading newspapers about the time when they were reporting my first fall, my taking the quarter of a million. A mouthpiece is a lawyer; sure, but he's a special kind; the kind who wouldn't take a legitimate client for anything in the world. A mouthpiece hates innocent people like a strip-teaser hates the hives. A mouthpiece is an accessory before the fact, or an accomplice if you wish, more times than not; he sells layouts to crooks, plans for robbing people.

I made a note of the name, Tom Atchison, and his town, two counties over from Altonsburg. 'Sure,' I said again. 'We're going to make it. Today we go see real-estate men.'

'That's your department, Danny boy. You're the smoothie.'

So I was. I took the list that Mr. Oxford had had Mr. Jerome prepare, and studied it. Five real-estate men. We'd dug clay from eight deposits — Jerry Quarry said some of them were almost of commercial grade — but five would do it. I decided to commission each of the realtors to get me an option on one piece of property.

The first man I called on took the legal description of the property I mentioned and studied it. He was a fat man, neat in a gray gabardine suit, sitting behind a neat desk decorated with a golf trophy and a plaque saying he was Mr. Philip 'Phil' Dryslowe.

He reared back in his swivel chair. 'This land now. This piece of property. I'm not sure it's for sale. I . . . am not . . . quite certain.'

Exultation rushed up from my belly. The mark had fallen, the sucker had bitten! We had them. I said, 'Can't you find out?'

The realtor nodded; a fat owl in a gabardine suit. 'I have good connections in this town. Let me make a phone call.' He held the phone with an air and dialed with aplomb. 'Calling the county clerk,' he said. 'Personal friend of mine.' He grinned at the invisible friend on the other end of the wire. 'Larry, old boy. How are you?'

I had been a Larry a little while before. Yes. I had been Larry when I was Colomba's lover. But now I was Scott, and Colomba was Susan, and I was here to make money, not love.

Mr. Dryslowe hung up the phone. 'Yes,' he said. 'Just as I thought. That property changed hands a few days ago. Stands to reason the new owner won't want to turn it over right away, would he? Unless you were willing and able to show him a substantial profit.'

'I am not a rich man.'

Mr. Dryslowe laughed as though I'd made the wisecrack of the year. 'I doubt that, Mr. Read. And anyway, the people behind you, they have all the money in the world.'

'I'm a free agent. I don't work for anybody.'

He looked wise. 'Sure, sure. Want to make me an offer?'

'Fifty dollars an acre.'

That got a big hoot. 'About what the new owner paid, I reckon. You'll have to do better than that.'

'I guess I'll look up the new owner and talk directly to him.'

He looked as sad as a hound pup; he drooped all over. 'Now, now, dealing in land isn't like making dinner — ' He broke off. 'It's a specialty, and this is the age of specialization. Besides, you wouldn't want to do a poor country boy out of his commission, would you?'

I considered this. 'All right,' I said finally. 'Draw up a paper specifying that in this deal, on this land, you're my agent. You get the usual legal commission — five percent, right?'

He beamed.

We needed him, of course. He had to feed information to the mark about which land we wanted. He had to get Mr. Jerome hooked; we needed Jerome Oxford dead broke. Then, when we threatened to pull out and leave him with some worthless clay fields instead of life savings, he would be desperate; he would go on the send.

I was humming when I got back to the hotel. Jerry Quarry, in my room, didn't look happy. He waved a piece of paper at me. White paper, but heavy; some sort of lady's notepaper. 'Something phony, Danny boy.'

All it said was: 'I have to see you at once. I will be out all day.' It was signed simply:

'C.'

'This is from the mark's wife,' I said.

'That I knew,' Jerry Quarry said. 'But what's with all this? What's this 'C' business? Her name's Susan Oxford. You been getting a little on the side, Danny? You crossing us up for a dame?'

'No, no,' I said. Jerry Quarry could be mean and tough and dangerous. 'It's just that I knew her before, but I didn't know she was married to the mark. It's nothing to worry about, Jerry. She wouldn't want her husband to know about me any more than we'd want out mitts tipped to him. Quiet all around.'

He was still frowning. 'I don't like it. You better get out there. I'll get Chester or Grif to cover you if the mark shows up. We don't want any hitches now.'

'What could the heavies do?'

'Jump him if he shows up,' Jerry said calmly. 'Beat him up, give you and the dame time to get your clothes back on. Then she can say she heard a guy prowling around and called you to see if her husband was with you. You gotta let Chester get away, though; he can't stand a pinch.'

'You think of everything, Jerry. But there'll be no clothes taken off.'

He grinned his wolfish yellow-toothed grin. 'Man, you never know, you just never know, when a dame and a guy get together . . .'

There were no cars parked around the old house, no car in the garage. I wished I could hide my own car, but the place stood out in the open; there was no cover.

She answered the doorbell herself. 'It's all right,' she said. 'The maid's out.'

So I took a step into the house, and that brought me a step nearer her, and then she was in my arms, though I'd sworn nothing like that would happen. 'Oh, Colomba, baby, my God, it's been a long time.'

And she was clinging to me, and

moaning, and saying, 'How do you think it's been for me, with you here in town?'

My hands were all over her, and hers over me. We couldn't get close enough together; she was moaning, and I thought I was going to faint. We started to sink down to the hall floor together.

She said, 'Not here, please not here . . .'

And we went down the hall, and up the stairs, my whole body twisting with the torture of waiting.

I remember falling on an old brass bed with her, writhing on a white counterpane, getting to her with our clothes half off. It was fast and sloppy, done the way a couple of junior high-school kids would do it, but it was wonderful; it was the weekend all over again.

Then we were lying on the bed side by side, her hair all messed, my face covered with dried sweat. She said, 'Oh, God, oh, and I don't even know what to call you. You were Larry and now you're Scott Read and — '

'Mark,' I said. 'You know my real name.'

She sat up then, and poked at her hair. 'Yes. Mark Daniels. Who stole from his bank and — Mark Daniels, the thief. What are you doing to my husband, Mark?'

I swung my legs off the other side of the bed. We were back on the con again. I said, 'Why, you don't love him, do you?' That was just stalling. I was getting clothes back into order, smoothing my hair, tightening my tie. I had torn the top button off my shirt; I'd better find it before the mark came home.

'No, you know I don't love him,' Colomba said. 'But his money's part mine. He's taken every cent we have and put it into real estate around the county. Real estate he's going to sell to you. But you're not a big businessman; you're a thief.'

Coming from her, the word was a rawhide lash across my face. 'We're conning him,' I said. 'Sure. And when he's conned, you and I are going away together, Colomba. Colomba . . . '

She got up and went to an old high bureau varnished a hideous yellow. She took up a comb and started fixing herself. Her dress was badly wrinkled, though. I don't know whether it was their bedroom or a guest room; I never asked.

She said, 'I don't know whether I believe you or not. I — '

And there was a pistol shot.

She ran to the window and looked out through the lace curtains. 'Oh, Mark, Mark, Jerome's car is out there. I never heard him drive up — '

'He in it?'

'No; he's in the house someplace. He — you heard it — he's killed himself — '

There was no way of knowing how long I'd been there. Ten minutes, an hour . . . I'd been out of my head; time had meant nothing. 'Let's get downstairs and see.'

We raced to the stairs. I don't know what we expected, but what we found was Jerry Quarry standing in the hall, looking cheap and tough and as out of place as a minister in a crap game.

'Come on, Danny boy. We gotta blow. Chester's killed the mark.'

Just like that. Colomba screamed.

I said, 'Why, man, why?'

'Chester was in the house here. You know him; locks are his dish. The mark came home, he was going to go upstairs, Chester tries the heavy on him, and the mark pulls a little old gun. Chester takes it away and — it goes off.'

Colomba let out a little yelp and slid to the stairs. I caught her before she tumbled down them and carried her down to Jerry.

'Heave her on a couch,' Jerry said. 'We gotta blow, Danny. Chester's already on his way; he'll pick up Grif and scram town.'

But I only took half his advice; I carried Colomba to a couch. I bent over her.

'She's all right,' Jerry said. 'Her husband got killed by a burglar; it happens all the time.'

Even then I almost laughed at that one. But it wasn't time to laugh, it was time to blow; Jerry was pulling at my coat. I managed to kiss Colomba once, and then he had me underway.

He was muttering stuff like, 'Love, and we've blown the best big con anybody ever had.' We got in my car outside, and I started out. The cops could read the tire marks all they wanted; the car had the most widely sold tires in the country.

We drove out in the countryside a way, then parked to talk. The con was blown; the mark was dead. There'd only been a couple of days more before we put him on the send, into his father's bank. It was so easy: he'd bought the land, and now we would offer to sell out our own ceramic company, because we had the only clay deposit in the world suitable for making ceramic nose cones for astronautic missiles, or some other double talk. All he had to do was borrow a little money from his father's bank, for a day, and . . . It didn't matter. The con was blown.

I rested my forehead on the steering wheel and asked, 'The cops won't get Chester?'

'Hell, no. He and Grif will have scrammed. I hung around to warn you. The cops'll be looking into everybody and everything. With our records, it's no place for us.'

'Thanks, Jerry,' I said absently. But of

course he hadn't hung around to warn me; I was carrying the loot. We had twenty-eight hundred bucks on deposit in the Union State Bank, and I was the only one who could get it out. If we split it four ways, I was back down to seven hundred dollars; back on the make. Only this time, we didn't have a truckload of stolen liquor to play with. We didn't have anything but each other, and it began to look as though ex-cons were not the best company to travel with.

'Where did the boys go, Jerry?'

'Back to where they waited for us. I told them I'd bring them their dough.'

'You would? Not us?'

He couldn't look at me. He examined the walnut trees as though he was going into the tree business. 'The heat's on you, Danny. I'm sorry, but that's the way it is. They dig, and the cops'll maybe find out that you ain't anything at all to that clay company. They can't hurt you, a one-time loser. But I've fallen three times. Get a good mouthpiece, and what then? An attempted con — a year, maybe less.'

'So you're ditching me.'

He made himself look at me — not at my eyes, but at my chin. 'We talked it over. How much dough we got left? Three grand?'

'Twenty-eight hundred.'

'So give us five hundred apiece, and keep the rest. You picked up the heat fronting for us. That okay?'

It was amazingly decent. I'd always thought that honor among thieves was a cliché, something in a copy book. I said, 'The heat's not so heavy on my back. Unless they fingerprint me, I'm Scott Read, not Mark Daniels who took a rap.'

'You ain't been Scott Read long enough or deep enough. They call that ceramic company we wrote to, you haven't got a job, they never heard of you up to last week . . . You're in bad trouble, Danny. If I was you, I'd dig up that heavy sugar you got salted away and scram.'

'I haven't got anything salted away.'

'The papers tell me different. Every con up at the house was talking about it when you come up there. You took a heavy rap sooner than tell that bank where their money was.'

'That money was stolen from me.'

Jerry was right; he'd never make a con man. He was looking at me with so much sincerity it came out on the other side; completely insincere. There was no honor among thieves. They — or he; the boys might not be involved — had made a generous gesture to me so I'd trust them and lead them to my quarter of a million.

Jerry said, 'Sure, you can't go get that dough yourself. But you could send me, or one of the boys.'

'If there was any money. I took it, sure. And did my time for it. And somebody stole it from me.'

'Stole an old-fashioned carpetbag from you, with the dough in it.' Jerry shook his head. 'What a story.'

There wasn't anything more to say. I pressed the starter button and put the car into gear, U-turned on the highway and started back for town. 'I'll draw some dough,' I said. 'Some getaway money for you. The boys'll have to lump it.' He hadn't been going to take them their share, anyway. That was all the bunco act he'd been giving me.

'Pal, don't get to thinking that money is yours. Like you did with the bank.'

And then it was easy to believe that Jerry had been on the heavy all his life — holdup man, burglar. He looked heavy. He looked heavy enough to weigh me down. 'Listen,' I said, 'I'll send you more when it's cooler. If I go into that bank and pull all my dough, the cops are going to be worrying about why. And then I'm in the clink and the dough is, too.'

'Pull a thousand,' Jerry Quarry said. 'You've been living it up. They won't think anything of that.'

We were just entering the limits of Altonsburg. A thousand. I was getting off cheap; Jerry Quarry could easily wait till he was out of town and then make an anonymous phone call to the police. I couldn't stand fingerprinting.

Eighteen hundred dollars. People said you could live in Mexico for a hundred dollars a month. Maybe in eighteen months, my money would be cool enough to pick up . . .

'And don't get any ideas about the rest of the dough being yours,' Jerry said. 'Grif and Chester and me, we got connections. We know guys right here in this town, in any town you go to, who'll knock your ears off for a fifty-dollar bill, and wait to be paid.'

'Okay, okay.' I parked in back of the bank and got out, then glanced back. The heavy was out of Jerry's face. He looked scared, but not of me; he was staring past me.

I looked, and nearly laughed. I had parked at the end of a line of police cars; cars in black and white, with sheriff's and city police markings on them. I said, 'You see what I mean, Jerry? I better not take out more than five hundred.'

'You going in there? Hell, that's a police convention, the inside of that bank. They sure found out fast. The dame must have called them.'

'Sure I'm going in. You've got to get away, boy.'

'Make it snappy, Danny.'

Five hundred would be enough for him; no, three hundred. He wasn't a heavy now. He was an ex-con, scared of an empty police car. Me, I looked respectable; I had a bank account. I strolled into the bank like Mr. Gray-Flannel-Suit himself.

Cops, all right. Cops and guys in plain suits who were probably district attorneys. All of them clustered around Mr. Oxford's desk. The man looked harassed, annoyed, but not tearful. He was probably thinking that he could get a non-relative to take over his son's duties as bookkeeper for a lot less than he had been paying Jerome.

I started to write a check for five hundred dollars at the desk in the middle of the lobby. Then I tore it up and wrote one for three hundred and took it to the only teller on duty. Her eyes and nose were red, and she sniffled audibly as she counted out my money.

'Have you heard about Mr. Jerome?'

I said I'd just heard about it downtown. 'No details. What happened?'

'They — they don't know. They're bringing in a state bank examiner to see if his books are all right. But Mr. Jerome would never kill himself. He was shot, I just know it.'

She sounded as though she'd cherished a secret passion for the late bookkeeper. I contemplated this for a split second. The wonders of nature; that a dreary mouse like Jerome Oxford would inspire anything in anybody was a miracle. I finished being Mr. Philosopher and pocketed my money. 'Well, I won't bother Mr. Oxford with my sympathy just now, but give it to him for me when there's time. And to Mrs. Jerome, too, if you will.'

She eyed me with a certain sharpness. 'Oh, do you know Mrs. Jerome?'

'Mr. Jerome had me to his house for dinner.'

The teller sniffed, but it might not have meant anything, since her nose had been drippy before I spoke to her. 'She's very pretty, most people think.'

One of the men clustered around the president's desk was eyeing me. After all, I wasn't unknown in banking circles; the guy who'd lifted a quarter of a million. It was possible that there was an eagle-eyed Gus among those cops. It was time to scram.

Maybe I'd been a fool to come in here.

But I had money here, I wanted it, and I felt lucky. And who'd connect tile-and-clay man Scott Read with snitch-and-hide man Mark Daniels?

I strolled out, and didn't look furtive till I was near the car. Jerry was sitting there sweating, though it was not very warm. I held out the money to him. 'Get in and get us out of here,' he said.

'Okay.' I pushed the money back into my pocket, got into the car, and started up and out of the parking lot.

Jerry let his breath out in a long, ragged whoosh. 'Ain't you got no nerves at all, Danny?'

'Sometimes you've got to take a chance,' I said. 'You wanted your getaway money, didn't you?'

'Yeah, yeah. Listen, there's a bus out in ten minutes. Drive me there, willya?'

'Sure you don't want to go to the next town? They might be watching the bus station.'

'Danny, I just wanta get out of this burg.'

Fine, fine. I drove as slowly as I could to the bus station; I didn't want him to have a second more than he needed. Altonsburg was bubbling in its lazy way. Little knots of men were on all the sidewalks, and there could be no doubt what they were talking about: Jerome Oxford and his untimely end. And untimely it was; it certainly had short-circuited as neat a big con as anyone ever set up.

The bus was burping behind the station; I stopped in front. Jerry Quarry reached into the back of the car and pulled out his suitcase. I hadn't known it was there.

'I'll have to hurry, Danny.'

'Okay, boy, and I'll be in touch with you.' I slipped the roll of bills out of my pocket and into his hand. 'Tell Grif and Chester not to worry; the cops are going on the idea that the mark bumped himself off. They've frozen the books in the bank till they find out he didn't; that's why I could only get you three hundred.'

Jerry looked at me as though I'd shoved an icicle into his ribs. Fast talking was needed; I provided it. 'It's not a big bank,' I said. 'The police bookkeeper will be done by tomorrow, or even the next day. Hang around, and we can get all the money out.'

'No thanks. The heat's blistering my back.'

But the damned ingrate didn't even thank me as he trotted into the bus station. Three hundred dollars I'd given him, and not a word of thanks.

At lunch in the hotel, everybody was almost, but not quite, too excited to eat. My waitress brought me peas and carrots, though I'd ordered stringbeans, and two men upset their water glasses.

The fat realtor and two or three other men I had a nodding acquaintance with stopped at my table to ask me if I had known Jerome Oxford. Unkindly, I said I had, but I was decent enough not to claim having had dinner at his house just a few nights before. Social standing in Altonsburg depended on how well you had known the dead bookkeeper, and it seemed nobody had known him well. I guessed that his father had told him to keep aloof, as a good banker should. A banker with friends is a banker who might make an unwise loan.

Hell with this. My plan was to pull out right after lunch. I'd drive to another town, sell myself the car again, and open a bank account with the more than two grand I had in the Union State Bank.

There was plenty of cash in my pocket to last me till my new bank could clear my check, and no reason on God's earth why anybody should hold the check up. It would be signed, true, by Scott Read; but it would be made out to someone new. It occurred to me that up till now I had always been someone of English origin. This time I might try having a German grandfather; I might be someone named Schultz or Berserhammer.

Remember, I'd had a long, long time to study the technique of disappearance. The idea had come to me way back in my banking days, when I'd had to deal — one of my first executive trusts — with an agency that traced small-loan skips for the bank. The salesman — he called himself Vice President in Charge of Contacts — for the detective agency had been a go-getter. He had told me of hundreds of things that skips do to avoid being traced, and of the hundreds of things his agency did to trace them. Gradually a pattern had developed. Skips were all followed by one fault: they caused someone to lose money; and the someone went out of his way to make trouble for the skip.

But everybody, except Mr. Hill of the Good Cheer, that I had come in contact with had benefited. Well, not Jerry and the boys, at least in their own eyes, though I had converted a frozen truckload of liquor into cash for them. And if I had most of the cash, they had had a gambling spree that would have taken anything they had in their pockets. But Mr. Hill and the heistmen were too far beyond the law to go calling on detective agencies and police departments.

All my other contacts had been good. What state license bureau is going to complain about someone buying more owners' certificates than he needs? What drivers' license clerk is not aware that licenses pay salaries?

Mr. Oxford had had the use of some

money for a week or so for nothing; the bank that had held my uncle's cash while I was in the house had had even a better deal.

Of course I was being looked for, but I wasn't going to be found.

Now I was on my way again. I packed my stuff at the hotel and loaded the car. I remembered to tip the hotel personnel; I thanked the desk clerk for a nice stay, and I gave him the name of the ceramic company as a forwarding address. The only letters Scott Read would get would be from them, and they could have them back.

My actions were normal. A businessman who'd explored some possibilities in Altonsburg, reported to his firm, and drawn enough money out of the bank for normal traveling expenses. In the excitement over the death of Mr. Jerome, nobody would notice for a week or more that I was gone, and by that time they'd just forget about me.

The sun was shining, the weather was just right, and I was off. Maybe I'd move south; fall was coming. I decided my name would be Philip Heistman — in honor of Jerry and the boys. My car was freshly greased, the oil changed, the tires were heavy with tread. I didn't have a care in the world as I started out of town.

Then I repeated something I'd done with Jerry back in the city where we'd made the meet. I swung out of my way to see the place where I had last seen Colomba. In this case, of course, it was the house where she lived with Jerome Oxford.

Now that he was gone, she could move out of that gingerbread hell. Move out of Altonsburg, too; and wherever she went I could find her, since she wouldn't be trying to cover her tracks. Surely she'd inherit some money from the bookkeeper; he was the type to have bought all the insurance his salary from his father could afford. Maybe the salary hadn't been big — knowing Mr. Oxford, I didn't think so — but he had lived on the cheapest sort of scale. So she'd have money till I could find her and we could go off and live on my stake.

I was almost past the house when

something made me take my foot off the gas. There was a car packed in front, and it was one I had seen before; seen in the covey of cop cars at the bank that morning. This was no black and white job, driven by a uniformed cop. The only sign that it was a police car was the buggy-whip antenna and the tax-exempt plate.

A district attorney or a high-ranking detective.

This was the time to drive on, the time to scram, if any time ever was. This was the time to manufacture distance, and place it between me and Altonsburg.

Then I told myself I was the guilty man, fleeing when no man pursueth. Of course police would be at the house, looking over the scene of the crime, especially since they seemed to think that Jerome Oxford had committed suicide. Cops are very good on that, because their pals, the insurance companies, benefit if suicide can be proved.

I parked across the street and down a ways, where I could keep my eye on the door in my rearview mirror. And in about twenty minutes I saw what maybe I had expected all along to see. Three people came out of the house, and then a fourth.

First there was a tall black-haired man in an office suit; I'd seen him in the bank. Then there were two women, Colomba and a stout middle-aged dame in a flowered dress. Her hair would have been gray, but she'd brassed it up. Finally there came a state cop in uniform, with his hand on his belt, the way they go, ready to pull and fire at the taxpayers at any moment. The two women were not handcuffed together, but I didn't think that brass-haired dame was anything but a lady cop, a matron, something of the sort.

They had pinched my Colomba — only they thought she was Susan Oxford — for murdering her husband.

The mirror I was looking into clouded. My hands on the steering wheel shook with tension.

She wasn't guilty, and they wouldn't find her guilty, and everything would turn out just fine.

Of course, of course, of course.

The procession could mean many things. She could have sent for them, and asked them to bring her downtown to give a statement about her husband's death. If she said she was too shaky to make it downtown herself, they would take a police matron along.

But I didn't believe that. What I believed was that they were taking my Colomba to jail. To a dirty, stinking small-town lockup. And I believed she'd be there a long time; there's no bail for murder.

Her father-in-law would want revenge for his son's death, and he'd lash out at the wife, the widow, the woman who'd get his son's insurance money if —

Mr. Oxford would find out that Mr. Jerome had drawn out all his savings. He'd be savage when he learned that. And a savage bank president in a two-bank county has power.

I had to get her out of there. Because what I'd been trying not to say to myself was that I was in love with Colomba, and I didn't want to leave town without her, even for a few days.

She wasn't just a good shack job, or even an ideal lady to hide out abroad with.

She was my love.

11

These are the things that convicts ask new fish: who'll hide a man out in your home town, what dames are available night or day, and who is a good mouthpiece? Those are also the things that the boys in the house never forget. Some of them run remarkably stupid, but their memories are always good for those three things.

In the first fairly big town I came to, I looked up the mouthpiece: a joe called Tom Atchison. Jerry Quarry had told me about him. According to the bronze plate outside his little office building, he had a partner: Lepton & Atchison. But inside, the single door behind the beautiful blonde secretary had Mr. T. D. Atchison on it. Maybe Mr. Lepton was dead. Maybe Mr. Lepton was invisible, or upstate in the house.

I asked for Mr. Atchison, using all the answers that nearly twenty-five hundred dollars gives a man. The woman brought her crossed legs out from under the desk, and slowly uncrossed them. She took a deep breath. She smiled, and no dentist ever made better teeth. She laid the novel she was reading on the desk, and touched her hair.

She wasn't used to male callers who wanted her to hurry any of those processes. She said, 'He has a client in with him now. Whom shall I say?'

'You don't have to say at all,' I said.

Her eyes widened and she nodded, as though I'd made an important communication. 'You are a client, aren't you?'

'I'm not selling something, if that's what you mean. What shall I give you for a retainer?'

'Oh, dear. To — Mr. Atchison would slay me if I took a retainer before he talked to the client. He doesn't just take every case that comes along, you know.'

This statement lacked conviction.

She said, 'No need to stand there. Take a chair. Do you want something to read, or shall we talk? I'm bored to tears.'

'I don't need anything to read. Aren't

you indiscreet, admitting Mr. Atchison doesn't keep you busy?'

She laughed, at what I didn't know. It was a vague laugh anyway. She said, 'Oh, he's a long way past the bluffing stage. You know, young men who have to act as though their time was worth a thousand dollars a minute. He doesn't have to bother.'

'Then Mr. Atchison isn't young?'

'Oh, middling, middling.' She took another deep breath, and seemed to enjoy the effect on me. She said, 'I'll bet I know what you're wondering.'

'And what am I wondering, Miss Quiz-kid?'

'You're wondering whether I'm sleeping with Mr. Atchison.'

This was so much the truth that it started me coughing. I coughed till there were tears in my eyes. Through the tears I could see her gently laughing at me. When I had control, I asked, 'Well, are you?'

She shook her head gently. 'No. But there's hope. He likes to look at my legs, and when I first came to work here, he didn't know whether I had on slacks or shorts. And he patted my shoulder the other day. Yes, it won't be long now.'

'So there's no use my asking for a date?'

She considered this, chewing her lower lip. Finally she said, 'I should say not, no. Unless you're going to be in town just this one night, and it wouldn't mean anything and Mr. Atchison never heard about it.'

My eyes must have been halfway down my cheekbones by now. 'I don't think I ever met anyone like you.'

She shook her head. 'Probably not. I have an I.Q. of 158. And a law degree. Mr. Atchison is going to let me write briefs, after a while. But I'd be no good in court, you know.'

'I should think — '

'Only on the first thought,' she said. 'You don't look stupid. Men, a jury, would resent me. Like I was playing a dirty trick on them, looking like this. And women jurors . . . ' She threw up her hands. Her nail polish was untinted.

'Couldn't you — '

She interrupted me again. 'Wear horn-rim glasses and pull my hair straight back? Like in the movies? I look even better that way.' She turned, letting her dress slide over her nylon knees, and fished in a drawer of her desk. Sure enough, she looked better in the horn-rims; she didn't bother to pull her hair back, but I was willing to take her word for it.

'What am I thinking now?'

She chewed her shapely lip again. 'You're thinking that if the boss is smarter than the secretary, you've come to the right law office.'

'By God. Is that why you put on the act?'

She shook her head, looking at the doorknob of Mr. Atchison's private lair, said doorknob having started to turn. 'No,' she said. 'Mr. Atchison doesn't need anyone to front for him. I was just flirting, I think. Didn't you enjoy it?'

All she got was a gulp out of me. She said, 'I did, too,' and we both watched the door.

A man came out first, not Mr. A., since

he carried a hat and topcoat. He had the look all right; the look that Jerry Quarry had mentioned; the look of a man who has served his time.

He went out without looking at me or at Miss I. Q. Shapely, an indication that his trouble was deep and thorough. I put my attention on Mr. Atchison, the mouthpiece. About forty, give or take a year. Stocky, not very tall, deep blue eyes, blue tie to match, slight tint of blue in the gray patches in his sideburns.

His secretary said: 'This gentleman to see you, chief. No name.'

'Ah,' Mr. Atchison said. 'That's the kind you can ask big fees from. Come in and be fleeced, sir.' He smiled happily at me.

'Did you teach the young lady to talk, or has she influenced your own dialogue?'

He chuckled soundlessly. 'Has Nan been giving you a snow job? She likes to make young men wriggle. She always has, since she was about two years old. Earlier.'

Astonishment must have been written large on my face. He went on, 'She's my kid sister, you know. Nan, what have you been saying?'

'Oh, I told him I was on the make for you, and hopeful of getting results in their near future. You should have seen his mugful of dashed hopes. Then I told him I wasn't averse to a little interim diddling, so long as you didn't know about it, and his hopes rose like a balloon.'

'A balloon full of hot air,' I said. 'Shall we get to business, Counselor?'

He bowed and held the door for me. Shut off from Sister Nan, I could relax a little. I looked around the mahogany and walnut office. It sure looked like solid money.

The Atchisons were at ease in reading my mind. 'This was my father's law office. He was a very different sort of lawyer than I am; he rose to the supreme court of this state, and died full of honors and respect.'

'What kind of lawyer are you?'

'I intend to die full of money.' He flicked his hand around the room. 'This is what I inherited. This little building, free and clear, no mortgage, the law library in the next room; a house built in 1870, also free and clear but deficient in decent plumbing; and a baby sister to raise. I borrowed on everything that was borrowable, and got myself through law school, Nan through high school. Now she has her law degree, too, and the mortgages are off both houses. Look, I can't keep calling you 'you.' Give me a name, any name.'

'Mr. Timeserver.'

He moved his muscular body over and sat behind his desk, pushed his knees up against the edge of it, and rocked gently in his swivel chair. I took the client's genuine leather club-chair.

'I figured that,' Mr. Atchison said, 'from your refusing to give Nan your name. But it doesn't show on you. One fall, Mr. Server?'

'Right.'

The Venetian blinds were down — people would come to this office who didn't want to be seen through a window — but he stared at a window as though he could see out. 'I imagine — and I'm not being psychic now — that it was a pretty big fall. I think I'd seen your face in the papers, and they don't print your picture for going through a red light.'

'Which affects the fee, no doubt?'

'I intend to die rich. I told you that, Mr. Server. Want to tell me why you're here, or do you want a little lecture on the law first? The law governing client-lawyer relationships?'

'Let's have the lecture.'

He stood up, walked to the Venetian blind and straightened it, though it didn't need straightening. 'It is absolutely illegal for me to disclose, anyplace, at any time, anything told me by a client. I can stand mute before the highest court in the land and go unpunished. End of lecture.'

'Am I a client?'

'As soon as you make up your mind that you want this law office, and no other, to serve your interests, you pay me a retainer. Thereafter you are my client.'

I reached for my wallet and laid two hundred-dollar bills on his desk. He nodded, opened his desk drawer, and took out a pad of receipt blanks. He started writing, consulting a bronze perpetual calendar for the date, and then paused. 'There should be a name on this, Mr. Server.'

'Mark Daniels,' I said. 'And it's my real one.'

Maybe the fountain pen hesitated for a scratch; I couldn't be sure. He finished the receipt, handed me my copy, went to the wall, took down a picture of Salmon P. Chase, and masked a little wall safe with his head and shoulders while he spun knobs. He put his copy of the receipt in the safe spun again and replaced Salmon P.

'For your information, not even Nan knows the combination to that box.'

'Tell me,' I said, 'do you have Chase's picture there because he was Chief Justice of the Supreme Court, or because it's the portrait on ten-thousand-dollar bills?'

Tom Atchison sat on the edge of his desk and laughed. It was completely natural laughter, un-theatrical and spontaneous. 'Nobody ever asked me that before,' he said. 'Truth is, it was my father who hung that engraving there, I guess because Chase was a distinguished jurist.

Now that you mention it, the ten-thousand-dollar bill would mean more to me. But playtime is over. What kind of trouble are you in?'

'At the moment, none,' I said. 'But there's a woman two counties away who I'm interested in. She may have — probably has — been arrested for homicide.'

'You're not sure?'

'No. Her name is Susan Oxford. The town is Altonsburg.'

He was a real mouthpiece. He had it all written down and was on his way to the door almost before I'd finished giving him the name and place. He went out, was gone only a moment, and his blue eyes were sober. 'We'll have it all in a few minutes,' he said. 'I've got strong connections in Altonsburg. Nan's calling them now. Tell me more, while we're waiting.'

'If she's been arrested, I'll want you to clear her. Incidentally, she's innocent.'

His hands came out wide, palms up. 'Of course.'

'No, really. I know who did the job.'

Tom Atchison shook his head. 'That

probably is of no use to us. He isn't going to come forward and confess; and my guess is that your knowledge is not such as would put you on the witness stand.'

'No.'

He nodded. 'Let me make an educated guess. This killer is a professional criminal, and you and he were working together at the time.'

I took a deep breath. This was going too fast. 'Yes.'

Nan rapped at the door and came in before she was told to. She gave her brother a little slip of paper and went out again. Tom Atchison read the slip, then tore it up, fine, and dropped it into his wastebasket. He said, 'You are right. Susan Oxford is being held for a grand jury; suspicion of murdering her husband. But that's the bank family over there, isn't it? You could have found out from the newspapers.'

'I never read the papers,' I said. 'They're full of lies.'

'We all are, Mr. Daniels, we all are . . . Now, your interest. It is not just in abstract justice, is it? I mean, you aren't rushing to Mrs. Oxford's defense because you know she's innocent.'

'I'm in love with Susan Oxford.'

His blue eyes were marbles staring at me. 'You'd better tell me about the crime you and your friend were engaged in.'

'We were trying to con Jerome Oxford. There were four of us.'

'A big con. Grand larceny. A little more law: Anyone concerned in the committing of a felony is guilty of murder in the first degree if anyone — accomplice, accessory or victim — dies as a result of that felony or attempted felony.'

I leaned back. 'If you expect me to drop dead in terror, skip it. The big con never got off the ground. Stop trying to swell your fee and listen, and we'll all get along much better.'

He nodded. 'Forgive me, Mr. Daniels. I have dwelled among fools too long.'

'You don't need to know about the con. It's dead now, dead as the mark we were setting up; and we've scattered, my partner and the two heavies who were in it with us. One of the heavies — I don't even know his real last name — thought the mark was falling wise and killed him for it.'

'Impulsive of him.'

'Funny, Mr. Atchison. Funny indeed. The cops, as I drove out of town, were taking Mrs. Oxford into custody. I want her released.'

His eyes slowly closed and opened again. You couldn't say he blinked; he just closed and opened his eyes again. Then he sighed and said, 'I am still dwelling among fools.'

'All right. Have a good time with it.'

He shook his head. 'It is unbelievable. You went to this town to rob this man — con him, if you prefer. And then you fell in love with his wife.'

Put that way, it made me sound feeble-minded. I said, 'It doesn't matter, but it came up a little different. I already knew her, but I didn't know she was married to this mark. When I saw her again — powie!'

'Pow, as you say, whee! You knew her, but not her husband?'

'She'd given me another name. We had a ball together, just a few weeks before I went on the con.'

Mr. Tom Atchison got up from his desk. He walked around the office, his hands behind his back. He went and looked at Salmon P. Chase, who looked back at him knowingly. A couple of wise guys.

Finally, the lawyer said, 'Far be it from me to turn away business. Try and get your retainer back! But I had hoped that you'd come to me on another matter. Mr. Daniels, you are throwing your money away! You say you love this woman, but you were not completely indifferent to my sister before.'

'Oh, every man my age likes pretty women. But this is something different. This is for keeps.'

'You picked this woman up under a false name, and you had a — ball — together? She left you without telling you her real name, and it's for — keeps? That *is* different. She was married to your prospective victim at the time?'

I took a deep breath. 'All the things that you're saying, I've said to myself. All the names you're calling me, I've called myself. But in the end, it comes down to one thing: I can't live without her. It's that simple.'

'Simplicity,' Mr. Atchison said. He seemed to be standing back, looking at the word. 'Simplicity is the keynote of the entire situation. I asked you a question. Was she married when you had this so-called ball?'

'Yes, but she was thinking about divorce, she told me.' I knew I was sounding sillier all the time.

He whirled and leveled a finger at me. 'All right. I'll go over there and do what I can — and what I can is as much as any lawyer can. But you stay away from Nan.'

This was so unexpected that he had me blinking now. 'She looks like she can take care of herself.'

He dropped the accusing finger. 'I don't mind her being seduced. But suppose she married you? I don't want an idiot in the family.'

I began to laugh. After a moment, he grinned, too. I said, 'I'd like to see you in a courtroom.'

Then he was laughing, too. 'I'm good,'

he said. 'I'm very good. But we'd better not let this get into a courtroom. What did you and she do on this 'ball' of yours?'

Telling him was hard; it sounded sordid and grubby, and it hadn't been. 'We stayed at a motel,' I said. 'We went to bars and cocktail lounges. We took rides in my car. We laughed a lot.'

'The gay and meaningless gibbering of the lower apes,' Tom Atchison said. 'No, we'd better not let this go to a court. Since she stands to inherit a big wad of dough if she isn't convicted, and since there are always relatives who'd rather have that money, there are sure to be detectives to turn up the fact that she was shacking with a man a short time ago. And then — clang, clang, the gates of the state prison.'

'I haven't said her husband was rich. The family, but not the husband.'

Atchison looked at me like a housewife looking at maggots in the flour bin. 'You're an idiot,' he said, 'but not a complete one. Not complete enough, anyway, to try and con a man without money.'

Maybe I wasn't a complete idiot, but he made me feel like one.

'And talking about money,' he said, 'how much have you? It is what makes me work, you know.'

'Most of what I have is in a bank account back where we were conning.'

'Write me a bearer check — you know, one made out to cash — and I'll get it liquidated without leaving a trail from you to me. Let's see. You've given me two hundred. Another thousand will serve — for the moment, Mr. Daniels, for the moment.'

A hammer came out of nowhere and hit me behind the left ear. I'd walked in here with maybe twenty-five hundred; I was going to walk out with almost half of that gone. Then I thought of Colomba, and shook my head and managed to grin. 'All right, Counselor. Can I make it for two grand, and you give me the other half in cash?'

He nodded. 'In your spot, you aren't likely to bounce a rubber check on me. Anyway, you've got plenty of the nice green material.'

'I have?'

He sighed, a Solomon among morons, and said, 'You've got a quarter of a million dollars salted away someplace, my friend. I thought I recognized you when you walked in, and then you had sense enough to give me your real name.'

The time had come for me to be Mr. Cautious. 'There's no way of getting to that money.' It was the first time I'd ever admitted to anybody that the money existed. Tom Atchison had that effect on me.

'With the kind of lawyer you have now, you can do anything. Come on, write the check, and I'll have Nan run over to the bank and get you your thousand. I want you out and working.'

My time had come to look at Salmon P. Chase. He looked back at me without information. 'Working?'

'Get in touch with the real murderer, ride herd on him. If we know how the killing was really committed, getting your lady friend off should be a cinch.'

I had come to the right office. I wrote the check almost happily, though it just about halved my bankroll.

12

Jerry Quarry had said the boys had gone back to where they'd waited for us before we pulled the Good Cheer con. After I'd eaten, I shoved the car in that direction.

They weren't in the bottle club, but I hadn't expected them to be. At eleven o'clock I checked into a hotel, and asked the bellboy where I could get some action.

'Dames or gambling?'

'Gambling.'

He looked me over with that bellboy look that transcends race, age or color. Apparently satisfied that I was neither law nor Carry Nation, he said, 'I'm not sure I'd know about that.'

A five-dollar bill was the answer to that crack. Master Bells pocketed it like a vacuum cleaner in first-class repair. 'You don't even have to get your feet wet.' It was not raining outside. 'This hotel used to be first-class, with a carpenter shop to repair the furniture and everything. There's a crap game in the old furniture shop tonight.'

'Well, what are we waiting for?'

The flunky looked at me with almost as much contempt as Tom Atchison had shown. 'We're waiting for another five bucks,' he said. 'This isn't charity night.'

The way to the ex-carpenter shop was interesting. We got in the front elevator of the hotel; the bellhop pushed a button marked B, presumably for basement, and we sank to rest; then he pushed another button, marked S, and we sank a little more. Then the door opened, and we were being smiled at by a furnace.

We went around the furnace to its blank rear end and knocked on a door. A guy with teeth like a beaver looked out. The door was steel, fireproof, no doubt a legal requirement for a shop full of varnish and wood below a hotel. He said, 'Yanh?'

'Sucker for the boys to clean,' the bellhop said. 'He's got a walletful of the true geetus. Saw it when he tipped me.'

'C'mon in.'

When I turned to thank the bells for the introduction, he was very urbane. 'No trouble at all, sir. The guest's pleasure is mine.' Then he was gone.

The fire door clanged behind me. Fang-tooth twisted a deadlock on it and went to open another, lighter, steel door.

'You always go to so much trouble?'

'Naw,' he said. 'The heat's on in this town just now. Somebody took the chief of police's brother, a guy who runs a liquor store in a gov'ment town outa here. The chief's all on the side of law an' order this month.' He opened the inner door.

The room was concrete, floors and walls and ceiling, and lit by two clusters of lights inside baskets up near the top of the walls. A blanket had been laid on the floor, and the seven or eight crap shooters were talking low, but even so the echo was terrible. There were no windows; but two grilled vents, one near the floor and one near the ceiling, explained why nobody had suffocated as yet.

Jerry Quarry wasn't there, nor Chester, but Grif was on the right of the silk-shirted guy presently making the dice passes.

The only furniture was some cane-bottom chairs on which the hot shots had piled their coats. From the faces visible, no man had left his wallet or his petty change in his coat.

I emptied my own coat pockets and added to the pile. The room was hot, and indelicately scented with male perfume and hair ointment. I squeezed into the circle between Grif and the man to his left.

The point was eight. The man in the silk shirt threw a twelve and an eleven; I fluttered down a ten-spot. 'Bet he does.'

Grif said, 'Covered,' and laid ten on mine without looking. The man in the silk shirt threw a nine. The dice were high; sometimes they are that way. I was betting they'd stay that way, and hit eight before they did seven.

At once the dice started coming threes, fours and a single five; they'd gone low. Then a seven, and Grif raked in our joint twenty and a few other bets; about eight dollars in all. 'Let her ride,' he said.

He still hadn't looked at me. I covered twenty of his bet, the other gambling gents covered the rest, and he rolled out and crapped with snake eyes. We picked up our bets, and he hesitated, then reached in his pocket and laid down a solo ten. 'All I got,' he said.

I pushed the forty into his hand and said, 'The U.S. cavalry just got here.'

Now he looked at me. His face got absolutely blank with impact. 'I thought you was in — ' He choked himself off. The very name of the town in which his partner had committed a murder was poison to him.

'Don't worry,' I said. 'Don't give it a third thought. Roll the dice.'

He dropped the forty I'd given him, and money fluttered down to cover; I took ten of it. He rolled out an eleven, and was in business again.

But his heart was not in it. I bothered him. He spoke to the dice in the most desultory way, and when he passed them to me, he was only about sixty dollars ahead. Me, I was down twenty bucks, counting the forty I'd given Grif. I waved the cubes away and stepped back out of the game. 'I'm cold, gents,' I said. 'Not my day.'

Those eagle eyes knew I had left some money in the game; the only thing they cared about. Grif and I stepped back and out. He muttered, 'Let's get out of here.'

'Okay, Grif. I want to see Jerry and Chester.'

'You must be nuts.'

That got him a shrug. Fang-tooth let us out of the double fire doors, and we went around the furnace.

Grif opened a door onto a concrete staircase. 'You know your way around here,' I said.

'Me and Chester always come here to cool off. The chief of police is a right joe, if you don't pull anything in his town. How'd we know that damned liquor store man was his brother-in-law?'

'That doorman back there said brother.'

'Toothy? He don't know from nothing.'

We had gone up the concrete staircase; the handrail was greasy. Grif opened another door, and we were behind the hotel desk. I followed him around the desk and into the lobby. Two men with briefcases leaning against their knees were carrying on a low-pitched, intense conversation.

We went out into the street. Across the way was the hotel parking lot, and my car. I said again, 'I want to see Jerry and Chester.'

'You must be crazy,' Grif said. His big face was pale with intensity. 'Jerry's gone. Chester and me, there's no tie-up to that mark, and we don't want there to be none. And you don't want it. You're clear on the — on the — ' He broke down. He didn't want to say the word.

I said it for him. 'The slaying?'

It was a word used only by the fool newspapers; not by cops, not by heavies in their life's work of holding up stores and knocking out pedestrians and climbing in and out of other people's windows. So he didn't mind it too much. 'Yeah, we don't want you getting tied up to the slaying.' He gave me a greasy, unconvincing smile. He had my best interests at heart, nothing more.

And me, I had only his best interests at heart. 'Jerry Quarry said you needed money. I gave him some for you — '

'We never saw it,' Grif said. 'We haven't laid eyes on Jerry since we left — back there.' The name of Altonsburg was something he didn't want to say.

Still with his best interests at heart, I said, 'I was afraid of that. So I brought it myself.'

Of course. Jerry Quarry had given me a quick shake for whatever money I had on me; a short con, no more. All the blather about sending him more money had been front, saving his face; he hadn't expected me to send it, and he wouldn't have sent it himself, if our positions had been reversed. He'd had no intention of looking up the boys and splitting with them.

They had been necessary to his plans, as I had been. When the mark had come back from the send, we had intended to have the boys hold him up and take his money away. But none of us were necessary to Jerry Quarry any longer.

I reached in my pocket, got out my

wallet, and gave Grif two hundred dollars. 'It's all I can raise at the moment,' I said.

His little eyes squinted in his big face. 'After I split with Chester, it ain't much.'

'It's more than anybody else would give you.'

He nodded. He didn't believe in honor among thieves any more than I did. And it seemed dubious that he was going to split with Chester, though they were a pair, though they stuck together.

'You don't have to split that with your pal,' I said. 'You know who I mean. I've got two yards for him, too.'

'You can give it to me. Chester and me, we're a tight pair.'

'Nobody's tight to anybody else when there's dough involved. If you think he doesn't want it, skip it. I don't like standing in the heat any more than you do.'

Thoughts rolled around the bowling alley that was his head. 'C'mon.'

The car took us there. It was a high-fronted house, inexplicably narrow; it didn't look to be more than one room wide, but it stood out in the fields, nothing on either side of it, not even trees within fifty feet, and these scrawny, sad sycamores that no one would have tried to preserve.

There was a sorry-looking sedan parked at the back door, two slightly newer cars in front. We tramped across a porch as old as the one at Jerome Oxford's, but not in as good repair. Grif pulled an old-fashioned bell handle, and there was a jangle inside. After a moment, a black face pushed the lace curtains of the door apart, and then a very old African American maid opened the door. She had on a black dress and a white apron, but she didn't curtsy. 'Evenin' gent'men. Rest your hats?'

Neither of us was wearing a hat. Grif said, 'It's all right, Nolly,' and she trudged towards the back of the house, limping on bunion-swollen shoes.

We were standing in a hall; there was maybe six by six feet of space to stand in. Off to our right was a parlor with uncomfortable-looking love seats and straight chairs that had once been gilded. Ahead of us was a steep flight of wooden stairs.

Grif started up them; I went along behind. I was reassured by the fact that he was leading; he knew I had money in my pocket, and he was a heavy, and had been all his life.

Two rooms opened off the first landing. Their doors were open, and in one of them, two women in kimonos were playing gin rummy. In the other a naked woman stood in front of a mirror taking a sponge bath. None of the three looked up as we went by.

Good grief! An old-fashioned whorehouse. I hadn't known there were any left in the United States; I had never been in one before.

Two doors on the second landing, but they were closed. We climbed on; I was puffing a little by now. The third landing was smaller, mansarded and gabled in, if I have my Gay Nineties architecture correctly. Two doors, though; one of them, slightly open, showed a bathroom of unbelievable antiquity. It seemed to be the only plumbing in the house. I wondered what madness had moved the builder to place it way up here.

Grif knocked at the other door, two bangs and a tap. After a moment I could hear a chain rattle, a bolt snick, and Chester was standing there. He had aged, it seemed, rapidly and completely; his brown hair was white as a ghost's trousseau. But there was a towel over his massive shoulders, and the white came from soap suds.

He gave me a surprised look, which he suppressed as Grif dug him in the ribs. My heart thumped. The boys were not soothing when they got kittenish.

We went into Chester's room, his hideout, his cooling chamber. He had obviously been sitting at the bureau; there was a washbasin on it, a pitcher of water next to it. A woman, hennaed, short-skirted, low-bloused, was standing by.

Chester said, 'Fifi was just giving me a shampoo. Rinse the stuff out, honey, and scram.'

'You oughta have warm oil rubbed in after the rinse,' Fifi said.

'No time now. Gotta see these fellas on business.'

'Your hair'll crack dry an' fall out if you just use water.' Miss Fifi sniffed virtuously. 'You always oughta finish up with warm oil.'

'Rinse an' git.' Miss Fifi stopped sniffing. He bent over the basin and she poured water from the pitcher over his soap suds, rubbing vigorously with one hand. He shifted around uneasily, tucking at the towel to keep the water from going down his neck.

She put the pitcher down and reached for a comb and brush. Mopping his eyes, he took them from her. 'I can comb my own hair.'

'Aw, Chester, honey, I like doing it.'

'Scram. Come back later an' get your reward.'

She said that he said the cutest things, and got out of there. We listened to her mules slapping down the stairway.

Chester turned, not on me, but on his pal Grif. 'You outa your feeble mind, bringin' this lug here? He's hot as a Belgian pistol, an' you bring him — '

Grif cut him off. 'Our pal Danny here's got dough for you, Chester.'

Chester blinked with disbelief.

I reached for the old wallet, slipped out two hundreds silently handed them over. 'All I can do now,' I said.

Their eyes were busy casing the wallet, wondering if I was worth knocking over. I talked fast: 'It's a third of what I could get. Grif's got another third; I'm keeping one for myself. Jerry's out, the rat; I gave him money for all three of you, and he's lammed.'

Chester looked at Grif. The two of them shrugged with enough force to almost make a noise.

'There'll be more,' I said, still talking fast. 'As the heat cools down and I can get at our stake without getting scorched.' I felt like I was telling them about the framistan on the portis. 'Our stake that we got with that liquor-store shenanigan.'

They stared. There was a long, long pause — maybe almost a full second, about as long as I could stand it. Then Chester must have felt a drop of water thawing in the ice that was his brain. 'That's right, Grif,' he said. 'We had a big stake from that trick. It's nice for Danny boy here to bring us some geetus, real nice.'

'Why not?' I asked. It had been an effort not to let out a long giveaway sigh. 'You're my partners.' Like a cowboy on television.

'We could sure use some more dough,' Grif said, and we were in the home stretch.

'Maybe you'll have to move before I can thaw some more out,' I said. 'If you drop me a note where you are. Tom Atchison,' I said, and gave them Tom's address.

Grif said, 'You sure change your name more than any guy I ever traveled with.'

But Chester said, 'Naw, Tom Atchison's a mouthpiece, a square one. I know about him.'

'Right,' I said. 'He's helping me with the cool-cut.'

'A right joe,' Chester said. 'You gotta go, Danny? You wanta stop downstairs with Fifi, tell her I said it was on me?'

'Is her name really Fifi?'

'All the women here are called Fifi,' Chester explained. 'So a guy doesn't have to remember. You tell her it's okay with Chet; that's what they call me here.'

I said, 'I won't have time, but thanks anyway. You live here, too?' I asked Grif.

'Yeah,' he said. 'We both send some dough to Madame Ethel whenever we got it. Then, when we're hot, we got a place to hole up.'

'Take care of yourselves,' I said.

13

Tom Atchison was out of town, his sister said. She stretched back in her stenographer's chair. 'He's over getting your lady fair out of durance vile,' she added. 'Or springing your dame, if you want it simpler.'

'Good,' I said. 'He tell you about the case?'

She nodded. 'Give me a cigarette, will you, Mark?' So he had told her my real name, too. I remembered his elaborate play with the safe and my receipt. 'He tells you everything, doesn't he?'

'It's a beautiful relationship.' She held her head up for a light, and narrowed her eyes at me.

'My name's not Mark,' I said. 'It's — let's see — Leonard Fisher.'

'Len, I love you. I've been out of cigarettes all afternoon. That's the trouble with a one-woman office.'

'You could have called the drugstore,

ordered a malted milk and told them to bring cigarettes at the same time.'

She stood up, holding the cigarette in her left hand, holding her left elbow up with the the palm of her right hand. It was a striking pose, as I am sure she knew. 'A brain,' she said. 'Your lady fair is very lucky; she'll never run out of cigarettes.'

'Why so sarcastic?'

'Jealous, pal. I thought all the chivalrous knights were dead. The kind who'll devote their entire fortune, jeopardize their liberty, for love of a lady. Since there *is* one left, why couldn't I have gotten him?'

She had me silent, which didn't bother her; she liked to do the talking. 'Where are you and the fair Guinevere going to live? May-hee-co? Pa-ree? The Enchanted Isles of Forever Spring?'

'Lay off, Nan, will you?' It was the first time I had ever used her name.

She blew smoke at the ceiling, still standing tall with her legs apart, one hand holding up the other arm. She put the cigarette to her mouth and blew smoke down, this time at me. To say something, I asked, 'Where are the Enchanted Isles of Spring, for God's sakes?'

'Wherever there's a man and a woman and quarter of a million dollars.'

Then she looked a little scared, and went over and put her cigarette out in the ashtray. There was so much left of the cigarette she had wanted so badly that it broke and spilled brown tobacco all over the ashes in the tray.

'Your brother tells you too damned much.'

She shook her head, her hair flopping, and went to sit down, swinging her knees primly under the desk. 'I recognized you the minute you walked in here. Your picture was all over the papers a few weeks ago, when you got out of prison. 'Teller Finishes Term Without Disclosing Loot.' I read all the crime news; that's the kind of law practice we have here.'

'That's a lot of malarkey, like everything in the newspapers. I don't have the money. I had it, yes, but it was stolen from me.'

She blew a raspberry at me, something

186

I'd never seen — or heard — an adult do. 'Malarkey, my fine friend. Men don't spend money the way you do unless there's more in the hole.'

'You just got through saying I'm unique, one of my kind. Money is nothing to me.'

'Have it your own way.' She stood up, moving her long body in jerky, angry motions. 'This office has been open long enough.' She dialed a number on the phone. 'Hello, Eva? Nan Atchison. I'm shutting up shop. I don't know where I'll be; I'll call you. Mr. Atchison is out of town.' She banged the receiver down. 'Answering service,' she said.

'Fancy, for such a small town.'

'Oh, we're not so small. We have an expensive restaurant, for instance. Spend some of the money you don't care about on my dinner there, will you?'

'All right.'

'Well, don't break your neck with eagerness. I forgot — you're the white knight, the one-woman man.'

'I'd like very much to take you to dinner.'

She pulled her typewriter up, dumping it down in the well of the steno's desk. Suddenly her eyes were shy and womanish. 'You don't have to. I've got lousy manners.'

'You don't, and please have dinner with me. I don't know anybody in town, and I worry when I'm alone.'

'About Susan Oxford?' Standing, she snapped open a compact, looked at herself in the mirror, bit at her lipstick and decided — correctly — that she looked all right.

'I call her Colomba,' I said. 'She likes it better than Susan. It's a name she made up when she was a little girl.'

Nan Atchison wasn't laughing now. 'I used to be Rita Margarita. I guess all women do that.'

'That's what Colomba said.'

She stared at me. 'How long had you been — been out of prison when you met Mrs. Oxford?'

'A day or so. I met her at the first place I came to rest.'

She shook her head. 'You — you're kind of impulsive, aren't you? Look, I

188

want to take my car home, and leave it; I plan on getting drunk.' She grinned, her old self again. 'Also, I want to take a shower and change things. Call for me in an hour, will you?' She went to her desk, pulled out an index card, sketched quickly on it, and handed it to me. 'Map. I hate my dates to get lost.'

'All right,' I said. 'I want to rent a room anyway.'

'The Travelrest Motel's clean and close in. I'll call them for you?'

'I can get there as quickly as calling them. I noticed it on my way in.'

So we went outside and got in our cars and separated.

★ ★ ★

The Travelrest charged me forty-eight bucks for a week's use of a very nice room, complete with television and radio and phone. It was a relief to be back in modern times again, after the hotel I'd had to stay in to play Jerome Oxford for a mark, after the fleabag I'd checked into and out of to contact Chester.

189

I must remember to tell Nan that Chester and Grif might call, to keep on the alert for them, I thought. Tom Atchison had felt it important to know where the real killer of Jerome Oxford was. I'd spent four hundred dollars to make sure we could find Chester when we wanted him, leaving me a lousy eight cases. It wouldn't do to lose him again through carelessness.

I luxuriated in my clean, modern room. I hung my clothes up in the closet and shaved, though I really didn't need it; then took a shower and wrapped myself in a huge bath towel and lay on the bed, smoking a cigarette. There were still twenty minutes before I had to call for Nan Atchison.

She was a good secretary; her map gave me no trouble at all. But I was surprised at the building she lived in: a very modern apartment house, with lots of glass and vertical aluminum lines and sun decks outside each apartment. I had expected her and her brother to own an heirloom type of place.

An automatic elevator took me up. My

legs took me along a cork floored hall, and my knuckles rapped at her door. She opened it at once, grinning at me. She had changed to what I guessed was a cocktail dress or maybe a dinner dress, black and very plain, with nothing to distract the eye from the low square-cut neck. She walked across the room to a glass and marble table, the gown swirling expensively against her long thighs.

'Wow!' It was expected of me. Anyway, it came easily.

'Thank you, sir. There's martini makings here, or liquor, if you're one of the rough-and-ready type drinkers. Bourbon and branch, or scotch solo.'

'Martinis will do me nicely.'

'You make them.'

Standing at the marble-topped glass-backed modern bar table, I could look out on her sun deck, on the gardens laid out below. The highway, and my motel, were in the distance; the traffic hum was faint. Stirring, I said, 'I like your apartment.'

'You've just about seen it all. The bedroom just holds the bed, the kitchenette will take only a thin cook, and the bathroom's functional, to give it the best; cramped is a much apter word.'

'Apter?'

'Oh, more apt, if you're a purist. Stop stirring those things. Don't you know alcohol evaporates with ease?'

An olive went easily into each glass. I rubbed the rim with lemon peel, poured and carried her one, and held the other myself.

She said, 'I'm supposed to taste critically and say, 'Oh, good,' but the truth is I never had a first-martini-of-the-evening that wasn't good. Skoal, and rest your rear beside mine on this Danish piece of expensive furniture.'

'You're very mercenary, you know.'

'Aren't I just? Almost as bad as Tom.'

There was some significance behind the remark, but I couldn't make it. Feeling naïve and young, I asked, 'Where does he live?'

'He's got a huge mansion-type mansion out by the country club. His wife gets coded radiograms from Paris so she'll know where her waist and hemlines are, daily.'

'You don't seem to love your sister-in-law.'

'Oh, she's all right, if you like bitches. Make us one more, then take me to Felix's and buy me two more, a bottle of champagne with dinner, and some very old brandy with our coffee, and I'll tell you the whole family history and anything else I know.'

'That I can believe, after all that to drink.' I was enjoying myself immensely. I continued to enjoy myself through dinner — with only one more martini and burgundy instead of champagne — at Felix's, a low-ceilinged place that smelled of everything the French have ever thought of doing to food.

I had a good time. A man couldn't help being pleased, looking at Nan Atchison; I doubt if a woman could, either. And since she knew about Susan Oxford, about Colomba, I didn't feel guilty. There was no urge in me to be unfaithful to Colomba, and this big woman knew it, and we could enjoy each other's company without any sexual undertones.

We chatted — I don't know — about

food, of which I'd not had anything fancy in a long, long time, and of movies, which we'd had once a week up in the house. Finally we had the coffee, and settled for B & B instead of straight cognac.

'There's a place we can go dancing, or we can order more coffee, and they have wonderful Camembert here.' Her voice was lazy.

'How do you keep your figure?'

'Oh, did you notice that I had? Naughty, naughty.'

'Don't be coy.' The waiter came over and I ordered the cheese. He beamed Gallically, and we were alone again. I said, 'There's a redhead with muscles who's been frowning at us for ten minutes.'

She didn't look up. 'He works for Tom. We're counsel for half a dozen insurance companies here, and he investigates claims.'

'A detective.'

She shrugged. 'He has a very public eye.'

'That could be worked up into something.' But, putting cheese on a toasted cracker, sipping my coffee, I kept watching Mr. Redhead Muscles. He didn't look friendly. It seemed highly probable that he had an interest in Nan other than that of a fellow employee; and from what little I knew of her, it seemed possible that she'd brought me here knowing the detective would be here, and would be jealous.

He looked rough, though not impossibly so. I'd had a lesson or two in dirty fighting at my late abode.

Beside me, on the banquette, Nan moved her long, charming figure to rest a little more firmly against me. I thought, more fuel for the redhead's jealousy, till she spoke.

'There's Tom, my darling brother. And the lady, I presume, is yours.'

I turned, so quickly that a joint in my neck creaked. There was the lawyer, blue-eyed and beaming. There was a maitre d', bowing. And there, on Tom Atchison's arm was Colomba.

'That's her,' I said.

Nan turned her face up to mine without moving her warm body. 'You sound all choked up, darling. What is it you call her, Calpurnia?'

'Colomba.'

'No need to snap my head off; you've already eaten. They're coming over here. I thought maybe Tom wouldn't want her seen with you. Ahhhh . . . You'll have to stand up like a little gentleman, just when we were so comfortable.'

They reached us just as I got myself on my feet. Behind them, the muscle man watched curiously. Colomba was paler than I had ever seen her before. She grabbed my hand and said, 'Oh, that's why Tom came and got me. It was you all the time.'

Tom Atchison said, 'I didn't know whether you wanted to appear in this, Mr. — '

With an effort I remembered that I was, or was about to become, Leonard Fisher. I would have to go get another driver's license tomorrow and sell myself the car again. Maybe I ought to turn the car over, start with a new serial number, and so on.

Sudden fear clutched my belly, chilling

me; I didn't have that kind of money anymore.

I was still holding Colomba's hand. Catching Nan's sardonic eye, I let it go. I said, 'Mrs. Oxford, Miss Atchison.'

'The greatest of pleasures,' Nan said.

'Oh, you're Tom's wife?' Colomba asked. 'I've been wondering.'

'Wonder on,' Nan said. 'It's Miss Atchison; I'm his sister. But he's married, though not to me. Incest is against the law in this state.'

Tom Atchison clucked under his breath a couple of times, then said, 'We might as well all sit down.'

Colomba took my place on the banquette; Tom and I took chairs. He turned to the waiter. 'We've already eaten. Just drinks, and — a jar of caviar'd go well. With English crackers. Bent's or Bentley's or whatever they are.'

Colomba said, 'Scotch and soda.' Tom said, 'Two.' I said, 'Three,' and Nan bowed out with, 'Cognac on the rocks.' It was like the betting in a very rough poker game.

Tom Atchison took a cigarette from the

package I was laying on the table and sighed deeply. 'It's good to be home.'

'Rough down there?' That was Nan showing a sisterly interest.

'Not so far.' Tom stretched his legs under the table, looked around, saw the redhead, and raised a negligent two fingers to him. 'The prosecutors and police who were trying to hang the noose on Susy-Q here behaved as though they'd gotten their appointments for memorizing the most psalms of any boy in Sunday school. I threw a lot of Latin around, demanded the results of the paraffin test and the lie-detector test that they hadn't taken, muttered some dark things about false arrest — and here we are.'

Colomba said, 'They would have to let me go, anyway.' There was a sharp note to her voice that I had never heard before.

Tom Atchison seemed to understand it. 'Oh, the bill is being paid by King Fisher here.'

'Leonard Fisher,' I said.

'It doesn't matter,' Tom Atchison said. 'The thing was being kept out of the papers, by the way, if you care about having the lady's name smirched. It seems old Mr. Oxford doesn't mind having a daughter-in-law in the hoosegow, but he hates to have the family name in the papers.'

'They wouldn't have gotten it right anyway,' I said. 'They never get anything right. Only suckers read the news.'

The waiter brought the drinks, and a tiny jar of black caviar for Tom; it was set down in a block of ice, making it very expensive-looking. Tom said, 'I hope nobody wants any of this. It's my weakness; we all have them.' He looked from Colomba to me, not quite grinning. He knifed a few fish eggs onto a round, thick cracker, squeezed the tiniest drop of lemon juice, and ate.

'Ahhhh. Why do I work so hard when my wants are so simple?' He took a sip of his drink and turned to Colomba. 'You are not out of the well-known woods, Susy-Q. Your late husband's will has not been probated yet, but professional courtesy gained me a quick rundown on it. You are sole beneficiary, with no alternate named. That means, in case you disqualify, the next of kin inherits: Mr. Oxford's father. He appears to me to be the ambitious type.'

'If the will is clear, how can I not inherit?' Again there was that sharp note.

'The law is stuffy; it says that no one can benefit by a felony. Which means that if you are found guilty — murder one or murder two or voluntary homicide — the money will not be waiting for you when you emerge from durance vile.' He took his eyes off her and took time to smile at me.

'All right, Counselor, all right.' I had learned that he hated being called that.

His sister said, 'All this is very dull. I don't approve of talking law when I'm on a date.'

'A date?' Colomba looked at Nan. 'Oh dear, I'm afraid my — Leonard is quite a philanderer.'

'Don't worry, sugar,' Nan said. 'I hadn't gotten a philander out of him yet. He's very slow to action.'

'That's the last thing I'd say of him,' Colomba said. I had better learn to call her Susan; the other name had become uncomfortably intimate. She reached across the table and laid a hand on mine. 'I haven't even thanked you for all you've done for me.'

'But you don't think it was necessary?'

She looked thoughtful and she frowned, making delicious ridges in her smooth forehead. She was worth anything I'd done for her, anything I would have to do in the future. She was the most desirable dame in the world.

A knee prodded mine under the table. I moved my leg back and the knee came after me, no accident. So I pressed back, and pleasant warmth came up my thigh. I moved slightly, caught the knee between my two, and the warmth increased.

Colomba was chatting with Tom, something about Jerome Oxford's life insurance; he was saying he'd look into it. She never looked at me, and I wondered about women — all actresses, every one of them. I dropped my hand into my lap with what I hoped was a completely casual air, so that I could stroke that nylon kneecap.

And then I realized that Nan Atchison

was grinning at me wickedly. Hell. Colomba was sitting at such an angle that she'd have to have her leg amputated to put it between mine. It was Nan's knee I was fondling.

I tried to wriggle away, and a little voice inside me said, 'Don't be a sucker, Mark Daniels.' The knee moved gently up and down between mine, and my face got red as Nan's grin got wickeder.

She said, 'Did you go to college?'

'J.C.,' I said. 'Business and accounting. Why?' I was aware of my voice sounding boyish and sulky.

'Just wondered if you took biology,' she said. 'It's a very universal subject.' Then the knee was withdrawn and I felt cold and frustrated, and hated myself for feeling that way.

Colomba said, 'We came right to the table from the car. I'm going to go straighten my face. Nan?'

Nan nodded, shoving away from the table with the same motion. 'I think my face is on straight,' she said, 'but my stockings feel twisted.' The two women walked away together: Colomba small and lively and made like a Swiss watch; Nan tall and springy as a filly with a wreath of roses around her neck.

Tom Atchison said moodily, 'Why do they always go to the ladies' room in pairs?'

'Don't know. I never felt the need for company at a time like that.'

He said, 'I'm going to have to have more money, because there's one hell of a lot of dough involved. Old Man Oxford put a lot of stuff in his son's name, presumably for tax reasons. It all goes to Susan Oxford — if she's acquitted or the charges are dropped.'

'Why don't you handle it on — what do you call it? — a contingent basis? Where there's big dough? I've heard of that being done by mouthpieces.'

He didn't like the word. His brows drew together in a frown, his lips tightened down. I happened to glance behind me to see, perhaps, if the women were coming back; more likely to slip away from his angry glare. Muscles was still watching us. I got the idea he wasn't there by accident.

'I talked to Mrs. Oxford about that on the way here,' Tom Atchison said. 'She doesn't seem to realize she's in any jeopardy; she has no intention of putting out any considerable part of her inheritance in order to protect herself. I don't work for peanuts, Dan — Fisher.'

'I'm down below a grand, Counselor.'

'Don't call me that! Though it's better than mouthpiece, at that. Well, you can spare it. Tell me where you hid that quarter of a million, and I'll send for it. I've got the best connections in the United States.'

'Underworld connections,' I said.

Again he frowned, his muscles moving under the unpadded shoulders of his jacket. 'Who are you to get snooty, pal?'

'Not snooty, Mr. Lawyer. Master Attorney, Thomas Atchison Esquire, if you want to be addressed with form and charm. Not snooty at all. I just don't trust any crook, any time, any place. Honor among thieves is for the copybooks.'

'Yes,' Tom Atchison said. 'But look at me, mister. Fear among thieves is not unknown. Well, it can wait. How did you make out while I was away?'

'I found Chester, the man who shot Jerome Oxford. I don't know his last name, just Chester. He's holed up in town across the state line, in a brothel.'

'A whorehouse. Give things their right names. Chester, huh? Big bruiser?'

'He's heard of you,' I said, nodding.

He stared at me. 'Were you mixed up in a liquor store shuffle in Cedar Brakes a little while ago?'

It was my turn to thin my lips and drag my brows together.

But that didn't fool Tom Atchison. 'I'll be damned,' he said. 'That was a clever trick. From what I hear, Chester and the muscle he trains with could never have thought it up. You must have been the brain.'

There was no reason to mention Jerry Quarry. I didn't.

Tom Atchison said, 'I might have a use for you. It would help pay your fee. That is, if you're going on with this — this defense of a woman who doesn't want to be defended.'

'I'm going on all right.'

'Very sturdy, very stalwart. Maybe very stupid, too. You sort of picked her up, I gather.'

'All right, yes. It started that way. It ended up as an awful lot more.'

'You're a grown man,' Tom Atchison said. He reached out, took the silver coffee pot his sister and I had been using, poured a little coffee into Nan's cup, and drank it off. 'Cold as a stool-pigeon's heart,' he said idly. 'Did Susan tell you what she was doing in the town where you met her?'

'She was talking to a lawyer about a divorce.'

He nodded and fiddled with things on the table — silverware, glasses, a package of matches. 'She was franker than I thought, then. She tell you why she didn't go through with the divorce?'

I shook my head.

He spoke to the ashtray, not looking at me. 'She had put twenty thousand dollars into one of the Oxford enterprises when she was married. Which means in one of the old man's companies, the son was just a stooge. She wanted it back, with suitable interest.'

'She was sure entitled to that much, for living with that carrot.'

'Yeah, sure. I guess so. But sooner than give up her dough — and not so very much dough as all that — she went back to living with him.'

'Temporarily. Until the matter could be — '

He interrupted me with a short dirty word. 'Money!' was the second word he said. He made it sound as dirty as the first. 'We're none of us worth a damn.' He stared at the empty coffee cup. 'I read something once, I don't know where, about termites who learned to eat steel. We're rats who've learned to eat gold instead of garbage. All of us.'

Not Colomba, I thought. Maybe Susan Oxford, but not Colomba. There were two people inside her exquisitely made body: Colomba, my lover, with whom I'd been in paradise, in Arcady, in Elysian fields; and Susan Oxford, who had married and lived with Mr. Bookkeeper. But I had better sense than to say any of that to a lawyer, a mouthpiece.

The women were coming back, Colomba first, Nan Atchison tall behind her. Tom Atchison made the scrambling motions of a man who wishes to give the impression of rising politely, but who hopes he'll be out-speeded; that the ladies will be in their seats before he can get out of his. Nan reached out, I saw her do it, and held Colomba back, so Tom had to unkink his sturdy legs and stand fully upright.

When we were all seated again, he raised a hand, and one of the waiters scuttled docilely up. 'A round around,' Tom said. 'My treat. Everything else is on Mr. Leonard Fisher here.'

We told the waiter what we wanted and he went away. Tom turned his head to the bar and signaled Red with a wave of his chin. Red came over. 'This is Mrs. Susan Oxford,' Tom said, not looking at his man. 'A client. When we've had our drink, I want you to drive her downtown. See she checks into the YWCA.'

Red nodded, his small green eyes gleaming.

Mr. Counselor still didn't look at him.

'Get that look off your face, Red. No passes on the way. The YW, you hear?'

Colomba and I both said, 'I thought — '

We were clients. Mr. Counselor bothered to look at us, first me, then Colomba. 'You thought what? That you'd spend the time from now till then in the hay, rutting together? Not so, friends. Tom Atchison's client goes into court clean as a vestal virgin.'

Nan Atchison drawled, 'If I remember my ancient history, some of them — '

Her brother snapped her off. 'End of joke period,' he said. 'The happy hour is finished.'

The waiter brought our drinks. I sipped mine while Colomba put down a stinger and then rose obediently. She looked at the three of us — me standing, the Atchisons seated — and said, 'Well, good night,' and went off demure alongside the redhead. He hadn't said a word.

I watched her go, my eyes stinging, as though I'd never see her again. Because I could feel both Atchisons sneering at me, I said, 'Is your heavy boy a deaf-mute, Tom?'

'Only when I talk to him,' the lawyer said.

'Oh, he is with women, too,' Nan Atchison said. 'He grabs, he doesn't ask.'

'I'll bet you know,' her brother said.

'Well, I'm very attractive, after all. I take grabs as compliments.'

'And compliments as grabs.'

They were about to fight. I faked a laugh and said, 'Brother or no brother, Nan is still my dinner date.'

'Then hop up to that hygienic roost of hers and into her bed,' Tom said. 'You guys just out of the pen are all horny, I understand.'

Nan was a big woman, with a big hand; there was leverage in her long arm. The crack of her palm in her brother's face was distinctly heard all over Felix's French restaurant.

Tom gripped the edge of the table so hard that the cloth crawled towards him a good three inches; I grabbed my highball just in time. Colomba's nearly empty glass toppled over and rolled on the white linen, leaving a shining crescent-shaped stain.

Finally, he relaxed and managed a smile. 'If you weren't so damned smart,' he said, 'I'd fire you, sister dear.' He shoved away and stood up, looked from one to the other of us, and turned on his heel.

He had forgotten about the round he'd ordered; it was on my check. The whole thing came to fifty-eight dollars, plus tax, plus tip.

14

Nan and I drove back to her apartment in silence. The lobby door was locked but her apartment key opened it. I held the heavy door for her and walked her to the automatic elevator. She said, 'You don't have to come up with me.'

'I'd rather. That front door system doesn't mean a thing; anybody who wanted to get in here could.'

She laughed nervously. 'Oh, I shouldn't be afraid, an old slugger like me. One-two Atchison, they call me.'

Her voice was so miserable that I knew she didn't want me to go on with it, to try and make a joke of that awful scene in the restaurant. I followed her into the elevator, pushed the button for her floor, and we rode up, mounting in a mounting silence.

At the door of her apartment, she said, 'Would you like to come in for a nightcap?'

'No, thanks. It's late.'

She shook her bright blonde head as though to clear it. 'I'm not just being polite. I'd take it as a favor. I don't want to be alone just yet.'

'Of course, then.' I opened the door for her, laid the key on the little glass table next to the door, and went to look out the window. She went away into the bedroom for a few moments, and came back, and I turned. She had the same clothes on, but she'd washed her make-up off.

'Make us two drinks,' she said. 'There's all kinds of liquor where you got the martini makings from. That was quite a while ago.'

'But I still remember.'

She sat down on the sponge rubber slab that passes for a sofa in a modern home. I mixed two brandies and soda, and took them over to her. I guess I bowed a little as I handed her hers. She said, 'You're very polite, aren't you?' and made a little gesture for me to sit next to her.

When I did, she put her head on my shoulder, and left it there while she took her first sip of drink. Then she set down the glass on the glass coffee table and swung her long legs up to rest alongside it, quietly handling her skirt so it stayed decently down. 'I'm sorry about teasing you before,' she said.

'Must say I enjoyed it.'

'Very gallant.' Her head lolled sleepily on my shoulder. 'I ought to let you go to your motel and get some sleep.'

'I've nothing to do tomorrow.' Or the next day, or any day after that. I was just waiting till my money cooled and I could go get it and life could start, life with Colomba.

She said, 'You're a complete rarity, you know that?'

'How come?' Night had gentled the traffic on the distant freeway; it had a soothing hum to it now.

'The one-woman man. The all-for-love, and damn the torpedoes act. It isn't done any more. Nowadays guys marry women who have money, or whose fathers have a liquor license, or maybe — oh, hell, sucker. Go home, will you?'

She sat up straight, jumped off the

couch, and started walking around. She had kicked off her shoes, which makes all but the very tallest women look fragile and helpless.

'What are you mad about, Nan?'

She shook her head. 'There's no use talking to you. Just go home, sucker.'

So I did. By the time I was at the door, she had disappeared into the bedroom; but just before I got out altogether, she stuck her head out. 'Thanks for the dinner. You're a magnificent host, and I'm a bitch.'

'Negative on both counts.'

She laughed and shut the bedroom door. I made sure the spring latch was on and shut the hall door, went down into the automatic elevator, and drove back to the Travelrest, and entered my nice, cheerful, modern room, feeling like a squirrel whose cage has a broken ball bearing. Then I slipped out of my coat, threw my tie on a chair and stripped my shirt off. I got a rough towel from the bathroom and dry-scrubbed my chest and neck, which itched for some reason or other.

And then someone knocked on the door of my room.

No one knew I was here except Nan, who wouldn't phone at this hour; and motel people don't bother guests. I stared, not sure whether to answer or not.

The decision was taken out of my hands. The knob turned slowly, the door opened, and Jerry Quarry walked in. There was a grin on his coarse face, under his slicked-down hair. He had acquired a sunburn someplace, tan rather than red. Probably been gambling in Florida, maybe Nevada . . .

He said, 'Hi, pal. Surprise, Danny, surprise.'

'How the hell — '

He made a sharp gesture with his hand. 'No great trouble. Chester told me what town you was in, and I coasted all over hell and gone looking for your car. So what if I don't see it driving in five minutes ago. So I'm checked in across the court from you now. Like the chaplain at reform school used to say, you are not alone.'

'Chester tell you where I was?'

'Yeah . . . I went broke.' He shook his head, laughing at himself. 'I had the dice, an' they hadn't naturaled since I don't know when, so I shot the load. And crapped out.'

'Florida?'

'Arkansas,' he said. 'It don't matter. I gotta get a stake. How much you got?'

I shook my head.

He was snarling: 'You was loaded when you went to see Chester and Grif. My dough. I need a stake! There's a mouthpiece will sell me a house. It's a good one!'

'A house?'

'A layout. Big politician. No squawk; he couldn't tell where he got the dough. A crook. He takes from anybody wants his vote — a state senator. This mouthpiece, he's got the plan, the floor plan, the timing, everything; even the name of the dog. I wanna buy it! I *gotta* buy it; I'm broke.'

Stalling for time, I asked him if he was taking Chester and Grif on this.

He stared above my head. 'Danny, I don't know.' He had calmed down. 'I need another guy; I didn't mention it to them. They're too heavy for me. Life, okay, if I get caught; but in that state, they still hang you. That I wouldn't like.'

It was the understatement of the year. There was about seven hundred and fifty dollars left in my wallet. I hadn't figured out what I'd do when it was gone. But not this. There were a dozen cons. They took time and a little capital, but that I had.

'Sorry, Jerry. If a hundred dollars will do you any good, I've got two C's I'll split with you.'

'Only two C's, and you give those heavies that much each?'

'So I'm a square.'

He came across the room at me, fast. He was a heavy, and I was a brain, but I was taller and younger than he was. And I still had my shoes on. I swung back on the edge of the bed, got both my feet up, and kicked. He went sliding across the motel room and ended up against the drapes along the edge of the Venetian-blinded window. It was sheer luck he didn't pull the blinds down and make a real racket.

The blackjack was half out of his pocket. I followed up, got my foot on his hand, and put all my weight on it; then I had the sap. It was a nice one, woven leather over what felt like sand. I'd never touched one before. I threw it behind me on the bed and hauled him to his feet by his bunched shirt.

'Don't ever try to rough me, Jerry. I'm a good guy, and I level with my pals, but nobody roughs me.'

Nothing like a gun bulged any of his surfaces. I shoved him away to go stumbling into a chair.

'By God!' he said. 'You're growin' up, Danny.'

'Just don't try to crowd me. I'll see my mouthpiece tomorrow; he may be able to get a little more money out of the plant we were conning. If he can, it's a stake for you.'

'You grubstake me, I'll cut you in for forty percent,' he said. 'Sixty-forty, right down the line, an' I do all the work.'

His face was a masterpiece of insincerity. But I had to pretend to fall for it.

'Sure,' I said. 'That's a fine deal, Jerry. I'll break my neck to get you the stake.'

He swallowed, rubbing the belly I'd kicked with the hand I'd stepped on. 'O.K. Just don't get too smart, Danny. You're a real brain, and I never worked with a head before. Five hundred, this mouthpiece wants for the layout. And it'll maybe cost me another note to bail out a guy to help me, to buy tools and all. You always got to bail these guys out; they owe for a hideout, they miss on the crap table or the cards.'

Having just crapped out in Arkansas, I couldn't see what he had to be so snooty about. But I said, 'Go to bed, Jerry.'

'I split my last ten-spot for the room here.'

I gave him fifty. He went away, his cheap meaty face happy. He had walking-around money and a pal who could get him more. A pal, or a mark? Jerry Quarry'd be most happy when he had somebody on the hook, wriggling; he'd have no faith in friendship, only in power.

There was liquor in my bottle, but I didn't want a drink. I got out my wallet and counted my money. It totaled a little over seven hundred.

15

Morning came; it always does. This one was watery and chill. The low-hanging clouds kept down the smoke from the factories, and you could smell it; sulfuric and rank. When I used the phone booth, the YWCA had no Mrs. Oxford registered. She had used a false name, I supposed.

Shave, shower, eat a breakfast that lies like battery acid in your stomach; get your car out, see that it is filled with gas, drive around to Tom Atchison's office.

But the office wasn't open yet. Nan was still in her modern flat; Tom was still out in his house by the country club — the house I'd never seen, with the wife Nan didn't like, the wife I had never seen.

And never would see. I was not the sort of client Tom Atchison would take home. It was surprising that his sister had gone out with me. But she was different — more curiosity, less ambition.

Then I remembered that the car was still in an old name, not the Leonard Fisher I had now become. I found an outdoor phone booth and used the directory to look up license bureaus, then used the directory map to find the nearest one. State offices open early; so they can close early, I guess.

There was no line; two people getting licenses, three clerks to hand them out. This was just for the driver's card; the vehicle registration was in another building. I took the application form to a stand-up desk.

It was no different from a half-dozen others I'd filled out recently. Name, age, color of hair, visible scars. I took it back. The clerk glanced over it and said, 'If you'll wait a minute,' and took it back of the counter, where a snappy black woman typed off the information on a form.

She brought the form back to me. 'Through that door, sir.'

I went through the door. The little man on the other side was a go-getter, a Coney Island spieler. 'Just this way, sir, put your hand there, and there, and don't help me, let me do the work for you.' And my fingerprints were rolled onto a blank. He put the blank into a slot and went on, 'Your toes there, and look at the light, and — zip, and thank you, soap, water and a paper towel there, courtesy of the governor.'

And my face, my fingerprints and my pack of lies about Leonard Fisher were all machined together.

This had not happened before. One state had taken my thumbprint — useless in the FBI files except in great emergencies. One had taken my picture, equally useless.

But now they had the works. There was no way of knowing if the prints went to the FBI, but they probably did; most full sets do, whether taken by defense factories, police departments or anyone else.

A few minutes later, the first clerk gave me a slightly damp photostat of my new license, took three of my dollars, and I was back in my car.

Nine-ten a.m. Very little chance of Tom Atchison being at his office. I drove to the

Vehicle Registration Bureau. They didn't mug me or print me. They just sold me new plates for twenty-three dollars. I had a filling station put them on for a buck. My money was still above six hundred and fifty, a respectable sum. I was all right.

But I wanted a drink before ten in the morning, and I'd never wanted that in my life before.

Tom Atchison was in, his office door open to the reception desk. But the big redhead was at Nan's desk, picking out a report with two fingers on Nan's typewriter. Tom looked up from a pile of mail and said, 'Hello, you're early. Have you met Mr. McGivney?' He nodded toward the redhead.

Red got up from behind Nan's desk. He looked more cordial this morning. 'I'm Mr. Atchison's dog robber,' he said.

Tom called, 'Entertain him for a few minutes, Red, while I see if there's anything in this mail.'

Red shut the door to give his boss privacy and got out cigarettes. He offered me one. 'Stranger to our city, mister?'

He wasn't asking for my name, but I gave him the Fisher one. I lit both our cigarettes. He said, 'You was starting at the top last night an' working down. There isn't a restaurant in town can come anywhere near Felix's.'

'You seemed to be drinking your dinner last night.'

'Ah, that liquor, that was on expense account. I et before I went there, at considerable less expense — and less comfort to my innards, too, I'll tell you. But I've had Felix's dinners, and man, they set you up. Make you feel like a king.'

'Too bad the expense account wouldn't stretch that far.'

'Yeah, yeah. But it was just an insurance case, and they go over those like an ant over a beef bone. Like this, it is — not much of a case: guy says he's a nervous wreck from a collision, has to go to bed at nine every night, can't eat good or sleep or so on. So I run into him, buy him a bunch of drinks, steal a glass with his prints on it, and write out an affi-david. This guy will drink so long as

226

you buy, and he'll stay up so long as he's drinking. All at once, no claim.'

I nodded. But I had seen him buy drinks for no one; all he had done was sit on a bar stool, holding his own glass, and glare at me and Nan.

'I had a fine time,' I said. 'Miss Atchison is wonderful company.'

The heavy redhead nodded. 'Yeah, yeah. I wouldn't know, too much. Not that I don't have a yen there, but she laughs. The princess and the peasant act, we play it all the time.'

Now we were getting poetry. Last night he had looked very natural wanting to separate my head and my neck; today he was doggishly anxious not to offend me, to show me that he looked up to me.

Tom Atchison came out of his office then. He took a cigarette from a package that Red McGivney had put on the edge of Nan's desk. 'Get on with that report, Red,' he said, and nodded to me. 'Come on in.'

I made myself comfortable while he lit the cigarette and hoisted his feet to the desk. 'Have a good time last night?'

'Sure.'

'Get anywhere with Nan?'

'That's a hell of a question to ask about your own sister!'

'Sure, sure. But if you don't ask questions, you don't learn anything. Well, the shop's open for business; what can we sell you?'

'Something besides the double-talk you gave me last night at Felix's. What are Col — what is Mrs. Oxford's status over there?'

Tom Atchison made a steeple of his fingers, then peered over it at me. 'Not good,' he said after a long, long pause. 'I mean, she's lucky she has me. She'll get off with life, and it wouldn't be that good if she didn't have the best lawyer in the state.'

'Great grief, man!'

He leaned forward, swinging his legs down. 'Didn't you know? She as good as confessed to me. You shouldn't have lied to me, Mark.'

My own name didn't move me to the usual protest. I said, 'I didn't lie to you. The heavy called Chester shot him. But it doesn't matter. I want you to get her off, squash the case.'

'Quash,' Tom said. 'The word is quash. Why, how in the world could I do that?'

'Buy some law. The cops or the DA. over there or the judge.'

'Why, that's dishonest.'

Blood rolled from my belly up into my head. 'Don't give me that, you lousy mouthpiece! There isn't anything crooked you wouldn't do if there was money in it!'

He turned and looked at Salmon P. Chase. Mr. Chase looked back at him coldly. 'Ah, true,' Tom said. 'I'm not offended by your words, but I don't permit people to yell at me; that will cost you more. And you're just about out of money.'

'I can get some.'

He waved a manicured hand at me. 'Do so, do so. The old jingle of the cash register stimulates my memory. I just might remember who holds the mortgage on the county attorney — not D.A. but county — on his house over there. A thing like that, now . . . '

'In the meantime, what name is Mrs.

Oxford registered under?'

'She's at the Y. But I can't permit her to see you. She must go into court like Caesar's wife, above suspicion.'

'But she's not going into court. You're going to — -'

He gave me a look that froze my lips. He raised one hand and held it in front of his face. Then he slowly rubbed his fingers together, the age-old gesture for money, folding money, rustling money. 'I may still have to go to court,' he said. 'You can hardly put bribery on a charge account.'

So I stood up. He was a young man, but when he put up the iron wall, you felt there was no use beating your head against it.

Outside, Red had moved to the chair I'd used and Nan was straightening her desk, complaining. 'Red, I wish you'd put a second sheet in. I hate to have the platen — ' She broke off. 'What is it, Leonard? You look awful.'

I was Leonard. But how can you tell a woman you're torn up because you can't see another woman? And that was what I was torn up about. Not the news that she'd go to the house if I didn't raise money, because I knew where money was.

Outside was my car. A few blocks away was the Travelrest. Jerry Quarry had told me what room he was in. I knocked on the door and after a while he answered it, clad only in violently colored shorts; his hair, for once, not combed, but standing up in spikes from yesterday's pomade. A black stubble and red eyes didn't make him any prettier.

'Yeah?'

'I got you your money, Jerry.'

His fingers made a noise like a distant brush fire running through the stubble on his cheeks. 'Yeah, yeah, what money?'

'Wake up, Jerry. The money for the layout. For the — '

His little eyes snapped wide open and he came awake. 'Shut up, Danny. Don't all the time go telling everybody everything you know. Five hundred bucks, you got five hundred dollars?'

'Yes.'

'Lemme have it. And about fifty for walking-around money. It won't take me three days, and you get forty percent for raising the dough.'

'No,' I said. 'I'm going with you. And I get sixty percent, for raising the money and doing half the trick.'

He shook his head groggily. 'Hey, I can't stand out here in my underlovelies. C'mon in, we'll chew it over.'

There was no window open, no air conditioning on; the room smelled of stale liquor, stale cigarette butts, stale Jerry Quarry. But it was where I could get the money to rescue Colomba; I liked it.

Colomba! She was now no more than a distant dream, a remembrance of bliss, of the best time I'd ever had. The woman that Tom Atchison had brought into the restaurant last night had been Susan Oxford; the woman I had seen as Mr. Jerome's wife was Susan Oxford; only I knew the living, wonderful woman who lived under Susan Oxford's crust. Only I knew and could bring her back to life, back to me.

Jerry sat on the edge of the unmade bed and made faces over his first cigarette of the day. 'Danny,' he said, 'this is no con. It's no heavy job either, except that I like a heavy along, in case it comes to a slug. But it's strictly for guys like me: a cut-the-glass-and-snatch-the-papers kind of deal. There's no room for a brain in it; nothing we can talk about, one way or the other way.'

'I need every cent I can raise. There's no use cutting Chester or Grif in.'

'If it goes flat on its old schnozzola, there'll be no dough to cut up.'

'Either I get the sixty percent, or it's no soap. You can cut the forty with Chester if you want to.'

'Damn, they don't make cigarettes like they used to.' Jerry snubbed his butt out, ashes spilling out of the ashtray as his hand shook, and he coughed. 'Danny — '

But I stuck to it. And finally he took the five hundred, and I agreed to buy what we needed — a good glass cutter, gloves for our fingerprints, and so on — and we were in business. Almost broke, but in business.

16

Another town, another night. A street lined with pine trees, or maybe cedars or firs or something; I'm no expert. There was a high wind blowing, and the light from the street lamps came and went as the evergreen branches bent and covered the lights and then straightened and uncovered them. The trees made a hell of a lot of noise, and I wondered why anybody would plant trees like that on an expensive street like this. But Jerry said it was all to the good. If we dropped anything, who'd hear us?

We had on sneakers, and heavy baseball socks over them; we were quiet as flies crossing the thick lawn, coming up to the side of the big dark house. 'We could go in the kitchen an' make us a mulligan stew, and who'd hear?'

'No thanks, Jerry.'

He laughed. The house had little iron balconies outside each window, for fancy, because who'd want to stand on a balcony just four feet off the ground? We climbed up, and Jerry was fast, putting a loop of plastic tape on the window and running a glass cutter around in a circle. Then he took a second glass cutter out of his pocket and ran it in the track of the first.

He rapped the cut circle with the handle of the cutter. The glass broke on the second rap, not clean in his cuts, but close to them, and in one piece. He hauled the glass out and handed it to me. 'Throw this and the two cutters down a storm sewer,' he said. 'It makes a bigger rap if you're caught with tools on you.'

'We're not going to get caught.' But I dropped off the balcony and strolled to the street. There was a storm sewer at the corner; the glass and the little tools went down it.

A police car went down the street — just cruising, no red light, no spotlight, no siren. I stepped behind a tree till it was gone. Another tree was between Jerry and the street; that was why we had picked the window.

Then I drifted back to him. I felt very calm, a workman doing a trifling job. Jerry already had the window open and was inside. I stepped in after him and closed the window. He opened it again. 'They can't see it from outside, and we might need a quick scramola.'

We hadn't brought our map with us, but we had it well memorized. Through this room — a marble-top table there, skirt it — into a hall. Down the hall, up a half flight of stairs. Door at the half-landing. Unlocked.

We were in a small room fixed up as an office. Desk, two phones on it, be careful you don't hook a wire and bring one clattering down. Portable typewriter in a case on the desk.

Open the case — my job — only slightly clumsy in my surgeon's rubber gloves. Take out the typewriter, turn it over. Behind me, Jerry was taking a picture off the wall, a picture of the Capitol Building in Washington.

Wait for the trees to bend and give you the light. There was the key, taped to the bottom of the typewriter. I took it over to

Jerry. It worked, a little stiffly because there was rubber from the adhesive tape on it. It opened a little steel door. Behind the door were stacks of letters and what looked like bonds.

'Junk,' Jerry Quarry said, removing them. 'You hold them. We'll put everything back. We can't fix the broken window, but maybe he'll think we got scared off before we did the trick.'

'We can take his silverware from the dining room and dump it down the storm sewer. He'll think that was what we were after.'

'You're a brain.' Jerry was feeling around in the back of the little shallow safe. Suddenly a second door came open; Jerry had touched the hidden spring.

A knob, and Jerry's glove turning it from memory. We'd gotten a lot for our five hundred.

Then the door was open, and money, lovely green money, was staring us in the face. I wanted to put down the papers I was holding and grab.

But that was up to Jerry. He picked up the first stake, and —

A bell went off. It sounded as loud as Big Ben in London. I dropped the junk I was holding and started out of the room.

'Walk,' Jerry said. 'Don't blow your stack, just walk.'

The staircase was wide enough for both of us. We walked. Down the half-flight, through the living room — watch out for that marble-top table — through the open window and out on the balcony.

We dropped to the grass. I saw Jerry stripping off his gloves as he walked; I did the same. The gloves followed the cutters down the storm sewer. We went behind a tree and stripped the socks off from over our sneakers.

A siren was blowing not too far away. I thought I could see the glow of red lights among the thrashing trees. Probably imagination.

We walked one block on the windy street, up a cross street, then down a narrow street paralleling the one we'd worked on. The sirens were getting louder. Jerry Quarry said, 'If they pick us up, what have they got? So we're wearing tennis shoes. So our feet hurt.'

'Our records.'

'No burglar tools, no masks, no gloves. No loot, damnit. So they hold us forty-eight, kick us in the belly a few times, and let us walk away. Not a thing on us. No prosecutor'd go into court on that.'

'Supposing they plant stuff on us?'

Jerry Quarry said, 'It's okay to be a brain, but don't work it overtime.' We had found another quiet street, and were using it. As the bullet travels, we were only about three blocks away from the plant, but we were working downtown all the time.

We made another block, and I heard Jerry let his breath out. 'They won't frame us,' he said. 'That dough is not supposed to be there. That big shot is the bagman for the cops; this city's lousy with gambling and houses and all. He picks it up, pays off the police brass. The dough's not supposed to be there at all.'

The downtown lights made the sky yellowish-red. 'We should have brought my car,' I said. 'How do we get out of this town? A couple of guys taking a bus or a train at this hour, it's a dead giveaway.'

'I don't like that word 'dead',' Jerry said. 'That's not a good word at all. Cop money, we were snatching for. They can't put it on the blotter, they'd never bring us to court, but — '

I waited, but he never finished the sentence. It hung between us like a dead wife's ghost at a second marriage. It was a quiet time of night, the movies not out yet, the dinner crowd gone home, but there was plenty of activity.

Jerry said, 'We hop a rattler, I guess. I ain't done it since I was a kid, but it ought to work.'

'Ride the rods?'

'Or the blinds,' he said.

'You are not filling me with delight.

He snorted. 'You're the brain. Think of some other out.'

I sighed. 'Okay, I guess we'll gave to do it your way.'

It was going to be a long night, and an unprofitable one.

17

There was a note tucked under my door at the motel: Call T.S. Atchison, and a number. I was staggering from tiredness, but I wove up to the phone booth near the office and fed coins in. A woman answered first — I guess Mrs. A. — and then Tom: 'Yes?'

No name. 'You left a message to call.'

'Yes, it's Mr. Fisher, isn't it?'

'Still.'

He chuckled slightly. 'Something's come up, Mr. Fisher, in connection with the case you're interested in. Could I see you tonight?'

'It must be two o'clock in the morning. I'm exhausted.'

'Nearer three than two, but it's very important. I'll tell you: go to bed, get a short nap, but leave your door unlocked; I'll drive in and wake you when I get there. It'll be some time. I'm way out in the country.'

'It must be very important.'

'Well, it is,' Tom Atchison said. 'Give me the number of your room.'

The maid had folded a blanket at the foot of my bed. I took off my shoes and tie and belt and fell on top of the spread, rolling the blanket around me.

The next thing I knew, Tom Atchison was shaking me, and I was coming up from a deep, dreamless black sea, with a bad taste in my mouth and my ears ringing like Lionel Hampton's vibraphone. Something intelligent like 'Muh' came out of my mouth.

Tom gave his light chuckle and went away; I closed my eyes again. Then cold water hit my face and I came all the way awake. Tom had gotten a cold washrag and was running it around my eyes and mouth. It felt good.

'Just a minute.' I staggered into the bathroom, scrubbed my teeth, drank a glass of water and came back. 'Okay, Tom. I'm awake now.'

'Whatever you've been doing to yourself, I hope it's been profitable. I need money.'

'Hell of a message to wake a man up for. How much, how soon, and why?'

He let out a deep sigh. 'Good. I was afraid you were going to tell me you're still broke. I need about five thousand, right away, and it's to bribe a witness who's going to swear — if we don't bribe him — that he saw Susan Oxford shoot her husband.'

'But she didn't!'

'Stop bleating at me,' Tom said. He went over to my bureau, found my bottle of whiskey, and took a swallow from the neck. He made a face and said, 'I don't go kiting around at this hour of the morning to get bleated at. I don't care whether she did, or didn't; I do care that this witness is reputable, and ready to swear Susan's life away.'

'You mean her father-in-law has bribed a witness and you want to raise the ante to get the — '

'Shut up!' He hovered over me like a hawk. 'What I want to know, and all I want to know is — do I get the money?'

'No. I'm broke.'

He threw up his arms, let them drop to

his sides, and swung away from where I sat on the bed. 'There goes the ball game. You don't have a phone in your room, do you?'

'No. Why?'

'Why?' He was very dramatic. 'To phone the authorities in her home town where she is. She's released on bail and in my recognizance, and she's recognized as my client. No fee, no client; bail canceled. Susan Oxford can get a lawyer appointed by the court; she may only get life.'

He turned and started out of the room. I brought him back with a sharp yelp. 'Good God, Tom!'

He turned and again flapped his arms at me. 'What kind of a world do you think you live in, man? One full of sugar and spice, where lawyers work for nothing, and judges are kindly father-images? This is now, this is real, this is for earnest. Oxford's the richest man in his county; his contribution to party funds could make a district court judge into a state Supreme Court justice, a county attorney into a lieutenant governor. He wants that woman convicted, and unless we have money to fight his money with, his wish is her conviction.'

'Five thousand,' I said. My own voice sounded feeble to me.

'Five thousand to start with. More, later; much more. My fee will be ten thousand, and I may have to pay outside investigators several grand. Say twenty-five thousand dollars, and you won't be hitting too far above the total cost.'

'I can say twenty-five thousand dollars, though not without gulping. But I haven't the vaguest idea where to get it.'

'I'm glad you still have your sense of humor.'

'That wasn't humor. That was plain old-fashioned despair.'

He said, 'Maybe the late hour and my own weariness caused me to act a little rougher than I should. But I have been trying to impress on you that this is serious, this is the showdown. I don't like to withdraw from cases, but I don't like — I can't afford — to lose big trials, either. And this one is surely lost if you don't get me money, in large quantities and at once.'

'But I'm broke. I'm down to eating money, and only a few days of that.'

He fumbled in his pocket, got out his cigarettes, offered me one. I refused and just sat there, watching him while he lit up and shook the match out; watching him as though he was a magician about to pull life and hope and happiness out of the cigarette package.

He went and got the straight chair and put it by the bed and sat down, carefully pulling up the knees of his trousers first. He cleared his throat and leveled his deep-set eyes at me.

'Daniels,' he said, using my real name with gravity, 'you stole that quarter of a million dollars, didn't you?'

'I was convicted of it,' I said. 'Yes, I took it.'

'And you still have it, don't you?'

'No. It was in an old-fashioned — '

He hit me across the mouth with the back of his hand. I was off the bed in a bounce, and flailing at him; but his superior weight, and maybe my worn-out condition, made me as dangerous as a still-blind spaniel puppy.

Tom Atchison held me by my upper arms, at arm's length from him, my toes just touching the floor. 'You damned little prig,' he said. 'I told you the time for fun and games was over.' He threw me on the bed, picked his cigarette up from the motel carpet, and started for the door again.

'It's still in the bank,' I said. 'It never left there.'

He turned and stared at me. I felt empty. The secret had been in me so long that it was as though it had become my guts, and now I'd disemboweled myself.

'In the vaults,' I said. 'One of my jobs was to relieve the vault officer from twelve to one, when he went to lunch. I used to put a little away every day, I — all that came out in the trial. How much I took, and when. You read the transcript of the trial.'

Tom Atchison gave me a most peculiar look. He kept silent a good minute; then he said, 'Oh yes, of course. As soon as I recognized you, I wrote off for a transcript. Yes, everything came out at the trial — except what you did with the money.'

'It's right there in the bank. I rented a box to a fictitious character and signed his name with my left hand.'

The lawyer shook his head. 'Pretty wonderful. How about box rent?'

'There are outfits that send mail from New York, or almost any point you name. A check is mailed for the box rent every year.'

'I see, I see.'

Now that I had finally let out the secret I'd kept in for so long, I could not stop talking about it. 'Bank personnel changes every few years,' I said. 'They use so many women who marry and quit. The top executives go out to lunch from one to two; only the peons eat at noon. In three or four years, there'll be nobody in that bank — from one to two — who really knew me. If I shave my head and grow a mustache, there isn't one chance in a thousand that I'll be recognized. So I walk in, present my key, sign the book with my left hand — and walk out with a quarter of a million bucks.'

He sank down on the bed next to me. 'It has the beautiful simplicity of genius. Sure. Anybody who stays with the bank from the time before you went into durance vile till three years from now will be in the executive group, the late lunchers. Damn,' he said, 'it's pretty. How about the key?'

'In the heel of the shoes I wore to prison. Who keeps your clothes safer than a state penitentiary?'

His laughter shook the bed, silently at first, and then raucously as he laughed out loud. 'Damn,' he said, choking, 'but it's pretty.'

'Thank you.'

This started him laughing again. When he finished, he said, 'Well, you'll just have to jump the gun. Even by now, there'll be few people in that bank who were there when you were. You served six years, didn't you?'

'Yeah, but — '

'Well, let's get going,' he said. 'Do you want me to shave your head or do you want to do it yourself?'

'Can't be done. My picture was all over

the papers when I got out of prison just a few weeks ago.'

'Newspaper photos — '

'We can't take a chance, Tom.'

He took it very calmly. He stood up and went to the door. 'Well, your secret is still a secret. You paid me enough retainer to make me your attorney, and counsel's mouth is sealed. Good-bye, friend.'

'Good-bye.'

He got to the door, and then turned. 'Even with a life sentence, there's a chance for parole in ten years or so. She might get it, if old Oxford isn't vindictive. He might even be dead by the time she comes up for parole.'

'Thanks.'

He waved his expressive hands at me. 'I'm not being sarcastic. Just realistic. With a court-appointed unpaid lawyer, without a little finagling here and there, your woman's good for a long, long diet of prison food.'

'You're so damned smart,' I said, 'figure out what I can do. I spent six years paying for that money in the safe-deposit box; I can't throw it away now. And if I get caught, what good will that do Col — Susan Oxford?'

'None,' he admitted. 'But if you're willing to talk it over . . . ' He came back into the room and sat down in the easy chair. Then he folded his fingers together and blew on them. 'We could get a court order declaring the renter of that box dead. I know a judge who — No. That would bring in a witness from the probate court or the surrogate's office, whichever you have in that state of yours.'

'Not mine. It's the one place I'm not going to go for several years.'

But he wasn't listening to me. His giant legal brain was working; you could almost hear it whirring. 'A lawsuit against your fictitious boxholder? No, too much publicity. The bank'll have detectives out looking for you, and they wouldn't open the safe-deposit box till they'd checked back, which would probably mean the same detectives — why use two agencies? And they — well, anyway, that's much too risky.' He sat there, shaking his head occasionally. Finally he said, 'No, you're right, it's just impossible. What good would you be to poor Susan dead broke?'

'None.'

So he stood up again. 'Her insurance money is frozen. Old Man Oxford had no trouble doing that; he's the big bull boss over in that country. But I don't think she'll get murder one; I don't think they'll hang her.'

'Hang?'

'Sure. This is a very backward state.'

Someone had just led in a mule to kick me in the belly, which wouldn't have been too bad if another guy wasn't slugging me behind the ear with a chunk of ice. Tom Atchison and the room went around and his voice came from a long distance. 'I thought you knew.'

All I could do was shake my head. The room stopped whirling, and the mule kicks weren't so hard; maybe Mr. Mule had lost his shoe.

I thought of going across the court and waking up Jerry Quarry, but what was the use of that? No crook would trust us with another layout. The best we could do was some simple heist, holding up a filling station or a liquor store. A few hundred bucks wouldn't help at all. This was first-degree murder that Colomba was charged with, murder one the boys call it, and in this state they hanged. Somehow or other the idea of a gallows was a lot worse than that of an electric chair or a gas chamber. I don't know why, now. Maybe I didn't know then.

Tom Atchison said, 'I ought to get some sleep. Tomorrow morning I'm driving Mrs. Oxford back home.'

'Oh?'

'It's always better — much better — to turn yourself in than to have them come pick you up. A good prosecutor can get the arresting officer on the stand and get all kinds of things into the evidence that couldn't be gotten in my other way.'

'Well — couldn't I drive her back?'

'Hell, no. If they ever find out there's another man in her life, she's cooked. Me, I'm not a man, I'm an attorney.'

'Oh.'

He stood up. 'I'd stay with you, try and bull this through, but there's nothing to be done; I've had my mind on it all day. Without dough to buy this witness off, they'll cancel her bail tomorrow, and she ought to be there when they do. I'll put up an argument against it, as her attorney, and then bow out of the case.'

'Okay, Tom. I guess I ought to say thanks for everything.'

He shrugged, came over to where I sat on the edge of the bed, and dropped his hand on my shoulder. 'Good-bye, fella.'

He got almost to the door when I stopped him. 'Tom — '

He stood there, swinging his hat impatiently against his thigh.

'Tom,' I said, 'I'm not such a very distinctive-looking man, am I?'

Tom Atchison looked as though I'd sprouted a second head. Well, four o'clock in the morning wasn't the time for a discussion of masculine beauty. He said tentatively, 'Well, you have an unusual hairline . . . '

'With my head shaved, with maybe lifts in my shoes to increase my height, with horn-rim glasses — would you know me?'

'I don't know, Mark. I just don't know.'

'There are three people in town here who know me. Col — Susan Oxford, your sister Nan, and a guy who's staying here at the motel, a guy named Jerry Quarry. Supposing we try it on them, and if it works — I take a swing at the safe-deposit box.'

'If you miss,' he said, 'you've done six years in prison for nothing.'

'Yeah, but if I cop — can you stall this witness till I can get back with money?'

He frowned, biting his knuckle. Finally he nodded. 'No. But I could do something I've never done before — advance my own money to a client.'

'Get going, then. Get down there and — '

He interrupted with a firm knife-cut of his hand. 'First let's see what you look like. To hell with Nan and your pal. And as for Susan Oxford, you're not going to see her; her father-in-law probably has detectives on her heels night and day. Let's see if you can fool me; it's my money that's going on the line.'

Before he had finished, I was in the bathroom, running warm water to get a lather up.

18

After I'd had breakfast and bought a pair of sunglasses and had the car greased and filled with gas, there was just a smidgen of forty bucks left. I went back to my room to get my bag. There was a woman sitting in one of the steel chairs in the motel patio. When I got out my key to open my room, she jumped up, and came towards me. It was Nan Atchison.

After my awful night, the sight of her was wonderful. I grinned and started to call her name.

But she stopped dead and stared at me. 'I'm sorry,' she said. 'I thought this was Mr. Fisher's room.' Her hands came up and beat together in a gesture of despair; tears came into her eyes. Whatever she'd wanted to tell me was important, but I had to play it out. The morning air blew on my bare scalp, the world was greener through the sunglasses, and I wasn't Mr. Fisher anymore; I wasn't anybody I'd ever been.

'I don't know any Mr. Fisher,' I said. 'I checked in here early this morning.' Then I leered at her. 'I've business now, but if we could talk it over at dinner time . . . '

She turned, her neat skirt whirling around her knees, and walked away. I was a weird-looking fresh guy and no more to her. Even my voice was changed; I had a rubber band around my upper teeth. That had been her brother's idea.

It was time to run. My bag was packed, and I left the key on the bureau; motels don't check you out, they just erase you from the room and rent it to someone else. Coming out, toting the bag to the car, I glanced across the court. The maids were cleaning out Jerry Quarry's room. He'd gone on the scramola early. Well, we had no more business together. We'd swung and we'd missed.

Time played on my side. Nan and the manager were coming out of the motel office when I drove by, but they were so busy talking they didn't look up, which was lucky. I'd done nothing to disguise the car.

This I took care of across the first state line; Leonard Fisher sold the car to Josiah Ethan, the name I'd rented the safe deposit box in. Nobody in the license bureau gave me a second glance, though I'd used this bureau once before, a few weeks ago, and though every time I passed a mirror I jumped, wondering what such a weird-looking guy was doing out loose.

Mr. Ethan — what a horrible name, but I'd been pretty young when I first picked it — got himself a driver's license and went to my old home town. Too late; the bank was closed to customers when I got there. Anyway, one to two was the hour; I mustn't hurry. I wanted to park myself across from the bank and watch the employees come out, but there was no use exposing myself to them any longer than I had to. No, stick to my old plan: one p.m. tomorrow, when the executives had gone to lunch. So I rented a room and bought a dinner I hardly tasted, and lay on a bed with my eyes wide open.

Supposing I walked into the bank tomorrow and old Mr. Bowman got up from the cashier's desk and said, 'Hello, Mark, what do you want?' Supposing Tom Atchison changed his mind about putting up the money to bribe that witness? Or supposing the witness wouldn't take a bribe? Or took the bribe and then testified against Colomba anyway?

Colomba seemed a long ways off and a long time back. The wonderful weekend didn't seem real. Nothing seemed real anymore, nothing I'd ever done but lie on this rented bed and sweat.

Just before dawn I got a few hours of sleep. Then there was the morning to get through; the endless black coffee morning. In a town where I'd once lived and worked and had friends, any one of whom might suddenly recognize me now.

If one of them did, would I take a chance on the bank? Maybe I would. What else was there left for me except to take that chance? My money was gone — the money I'd saved, the money I'd inherited from my uncle, the money I'd made conning the liquor dealers. I had to go on now.

At five minutes past one, I parked my car in the bank lot and slowly walked to the back door — the door I used to use to go to work in the morning, to leave work in the evening, to go out on the two coffee breaks the bank allowed us tellers.

I turned. Larry's Diner was no longer across the street; the clerks must take their coffee someplace else.

Going through the door, I was again a little gutless change-maker with nothing ahead of me but twenty-odd years of changing money and a pension. How had I ever had the nerve to embezzle a quarter of a million? How had I ever thought I could come back and pick it up?

Well, the smell of the bank gave me my answer. I was back in those days of furious, frozen despair; those days of knowing I hated being a bank clerk, and that I would never be anything else except a bank cashier, a bank vice president.

Yes, I could remember when six years in prison seemed no worse than six years in a bank, and the rewards much greater. So I'd make my move. It isn't very hard to steal from a bank, but stealing and not getting caught is something different. Me, I'd planned on getting caught.

To get from the parking lot entrance to the door to the vaults, I only had to cross a corner of the main lobby. It was enough; endlessly enough. A woman who would have been in high school in my time had my old teller's cage; only two other tellers were on duty, and one of them was old Mr. Phelps, who wore reading glasses in the cage and couldn't see five feet with them on.

Mr. Bowman's name was off the cashier's desk, and the plaque said Mr. Lyner. Mel Lyner had been a teller when I was; he'd come up fast. But he wasn't behind his desk now.

Right turn, and into the angle between the cages that held the vault officer's low desk. The plaque on it still said Mr. Mabty, but Mr.Mabty went to lunch at one. Another man had taken his place, just as I used to.

He looked up, and it was Jess Gulick, who had been a runner — office boy really — when I was a teller.

The mule kicked my stomach again.

I almost turned and ran. But Jess had seen me and was giving me the polite, void smile that bank clerks practice against the day they'll be bankers. 'Yes, sir?'

Go through with it, Mark Daniels. Go through with it and be forever free, free and happy with Colomba in some place where there's never any bad weather, or worry, or indigestion.

'I have a safe deposit box here,' I said. I took out my key. 'The name is — ' For a moment I couldn't remember it. There had been so many names lately. So many names and so many miles, and so little sleep. Then it came to me: 'Josiah Ethan.'

Anybody would spot a name like that as phony. But Jess just said, 'Yes, sir, Mr. Ethan. Just a moment please,' and reached for the card file, just as I used to do. It was the same card file.

He found the card, that efficient little clerk, and held out a signature card; I signed with my left hand. Jess compared the signatures, then said, 'This way, Mr. Ethan,' and we went back of the bars together. Down the aisle of the vault; it echoed just as it used to.

But now it seemed to echo not footsteps, but my name: Mark Daniels, repeated and boomed till I didn't see how Jess could keep from hearing it.

Here was the box; no different from all the others. It didn't glow, it didn't sing. It was just a box.

Jess Gulick used his key, I used mine, and the box was open. Jess took out the steel liner politely and carried it to one of the little booths where the coupon-clipping scissors and the pens and the blotters were all lined up so neatly. He shut the door of the booth without slamming it and walked away, his retreating footsteps echoing my name against the roof of the vault.

The money was still there. Five hundred five-hundred-dollar bills. No big bundle. I split it into five parts, one for each of my pockets. There were ashtrays in the vaults these days: modernity and liberalism had entered the bank. I took time to smoke a cigarette before I rang for Jess.

When I heard the footsteps coming

towards me, I thought: *Supposing Mr. Mabty has cut his lunch hour to thirty minutes? He'll know me and give the alarm and —*

Jess Gulick came in and said, 'All done, Mr. Ethan?' and picked up the liner.

I had to walk back with him; watch him lock my box again. To say I was through with it would be a little off routine; might make him look at me more closely.

Then we were walking out of the vault again. Jess muttered some sort of a good-bye to me and sat down behind Mr. Mabty's desk. He looked sleepy; maybe he'd eaten too big a lunch. He ought to watch that, or he'd be a teller all his life.

Now, back across the lobby. Don't hurry. Walk easy.

Back door. Open it. If they thought of it this evening, they could lift some very mystifying fingerprints around this bank: Mark Daniels Was Here, before or after Kilroy.

Easy across the parking lot, easy into your car. Key in the ignition switch. What are your hands shaking for?

Start the motor, put her in gear. No

one parked ahead of you; you don't have to back out. Easy, easy.

Turn right into the street, turn left onto the boulevard, keep going.

Drive carefully. You don't want to have to get your wallet out to show a cop your license; he might see the flash of green in your pocket. Fifty thousand in my inside breast pocket, fifty thousand in each side pocket of the coat, fifty thousand in each side of my trousers. Colomba, here I —

The city was behind me; there was the city-limits sign.

Trees on either side — there would be for a few miles — and then the suburbs of another town would —

A voice said, 'Just pull over to the side. Just nicely park the heap.'

Something was sticking in the back of my neck. It felt like a gun, but I couldn't remember ever having a gun stuck in the back of my neck, so how could I be sure?

Slowly I headed the car towards, the right of the boulevard. I pulled out on the emergency strip, and stopped.

The voice said, 'Switch off the motor.' And so that was what I did. The voice said, 'Just sit still.'

And that was what I did, too. A few seconds, a few years, an eternity or two went by, and then another car peeled out of the traffic and parked behind us. I tried to look around, but that thing was in my neck.

The doors of the other car slammed. Some men were coming alongside. Chester. Red McGivney. Jerry Quarry.

The voice from the back seat floor had been Grif's.

Jerry said, 'Out, Danny boy.'

I got out. We were a little group of men, chatting about nothing. Big bodies masked me from passing cars; eager fingers ripped my pockets empty of the five bundles. Red McGivney seemed to be in charge. He said, 'One for you and Grif, Chester. One for you, Jerry. One for the little lady. You'll take it to her, Jerry; she said that was all right. And two for my boss; he'll take care of me. Let's go.'

They stepped away from me. Grif said, 'Just a minute,' and they regrouped and he took my wallet off my hip.

'Leave him something,' Red said. 'He's

a hard-working mark.' Red's muscular laugh almost made me vomit.

'When you put him on the send, he really goes.'

Grif was taking the car papers out of my wallet, and the money; there wasn't much of it. I said, 'The little woman? Your woman, Jerry?'

Someplace that day Jerry had picked up a blackhead alongside his nose. It moved as he said, 'Long ago. She went straight and copped pretty with the banker's son — she thought. Then she got in touch with me up at the house: 'Dear Jerry, come and get me out of this.' I done so.'

I shook my head. Something like tears was trying to run out of my eyes.

'Don't feel so bad, Danny,' Jerry said. 'I heard a guy say once — you knew him, Red; old Professor Smoot, the big store worker — that the first dame a guy makes after a fall, she's like a waterhole in the desert; no water'll ever taste so good again.'

Grif slammed my wallet back on my hip. 'Let's go. Quit the schmoosing.'

'He's a brain,' Jerry said. 'He's a mark, but he's a brain. Maybe he could use the con himself sometime . . . Don't feel too bad, Danny boy. It was your first fall; you didn't know how it would be with a dame. You'll learn. Time you've done three falls, like me, you'll learn.'

Red McGivney said, 'Let's roll. We sound like a ladies' club.'

'But I saw her being pinched,' I said.

'Naw. Nothing against her. We got witnesses say she was three miles away, on the other side of town.' This was Red talking. 'My boss, he's a mouthpiece to end 'em all. Footprints to show it was a man did it. What you saw — Mr. Atchison knew you'd go by her house — they were taking her downtown because she called in and said a man was hanging around the house, and then she dropped the phone and made a noise like she'd fainted. They sent a cop; they sent a nurse.'

'But you really killed her husband?'

'What the hell?' Chester said. 'She paid me on the side; she was really sick of that guy. Who'll ever tie me to it?'

'You'll learn, Danny,' Jerry said again. 'When you've done three falls, you'll learn. You're a brain.'

Red laughed. 'Some brain. Mr. Atchison set it all up, so if the mark here wondered why he didn't read about the dame's pinch in the papers, we'd be covered. And then he never even read the papers. Some brain; he can't even read.'

'No.' Jerry sounded very serious. 'No, I never knew a head better than Danny's. I'd like to work with him, when he cops wise. Me and you and Susan, we could set up a good one.'

'No, thanks, Jerry.'

He shrugged, and then they were going; Jerry with Red, Grif and Chester in my car.

I'm a real smart mark; I got it before I'd walked two blocks along the boulevard.

A beautiful con. When I'd phoned Jerry, he'd phoned Colomba, or he'd phoned Tom Atchison who'd phoned Colomba. *There's a lop-eared mark at a motel on the highway. You've been looking for money to get away from that husband of yours; this is your chance.*

And from then on it had been a big con like all others. Let the mark make a little money first: the liquor store swindle. Then let him try and make some more, and see he flops. Then, when he's broke, put him on the send. He'll be back.

They could have waited in Tom Atchison's office. When a good big-con man puts a mark on the send, the mark always comes back. Why, even my first name fitted.

Pretty soon there'd be a town. In the meantime, I walked along the highway. Maybe I'd have to get a dishwasher's job to eat tonight. Maybe I'd have to flop in a park.

Yesterday morning, Nan Atchison had come to the motel to warn me. She hadn't been in it then; or if she had, it had disgusted her and she'd pulled out. There was one human being left; the rats hadn't covered the globe yet.

There had been tears in Nan's eyes. She had really cared about me. She was a beautiful woman . . .

I remembered her knee between mine.

I remembered her head on my shoulder. Any man would be lucky with a woman like Nan Atchison.

But then I remembered something else. Jerry had said that he and Colomba and I might go on the con together sometime. He'd meant it, too. Because I'd been a mark once didn't mean I was out for life. They were all marks for something, the wise buys. A crap table, a dame, roulette, the old liquor.

So I'd see Colomba again sometime. And if I couldn't take a woman away from Jerry Quarry, I was a lot worse off than I believed myself.

I began walking faster.

And then I stopped. I'd made my move; I'd gone on the con. I'd pulled a hot deal on the bank, a sharp short con on the two liquor dealers, and I'd kidded myself into thinking I was a big shot.

Only, the first real con men who had come along had taken me, whitewashed me, left me with just what I'd brought out of prison: five dollars.

Farewell to Colomba, farewell to the quick take and the fast talk. Some way, somehow, I'd get a job.

Hell, Nan Atchison would help me get one. And with her brother what he was, she was no woman to hold a man's past against him. She'd proved that when she cried at the motel in the morning, coming to keep smart old me from making a sucker of myself.

I turned, crossed the road, put up my thumb to fetch a ride. I was turning back, back to Nan Atchison, who could still cry like a human being in a rodent world.

Turning back, me and my five bucks.

We do hope that you have enjoyed reading this large print book.

Did you know that all of our titles are available for purchase?

We publish a wide range of high quality large print books including:

**Romances, Mysteries, Classics
General Fiction
Non Fiction and Westerns**

Special interest titles available in large print are:

**The Little Oxford Dictionary
Music Book, Song Book
Hymn Book, Service Book**

Also available from us courtesy of Oxford University Press:

**Young Readers' Dictionary
(large print edition)
Young Readers' Thesaurus
(large print edition)**

For further information or a free brochure, please contact us at:
**Ulverscroft Large Print Books Ltd.,
The Green, Bradgate Road, Anstey,
Leicester, LE7 7FU, England.
Tel:** (00 44) 0116 236 4325
Fax: (00 44) 0116 234 0205